ENTOMBMENT CHAMBER

I heard a little ringing noise like an afrit—a tomb spirit—might
be expected to make: dok dok. Metal against stone. I switched
off my flash and slipped over to the doorway and looked inside.

A Coleman lamp was blazing, and Brandt was kneeling beside it
in the muck and tapping at the wall with a little sounding hammer. He had his head cocked like a dog listening to an elusive
human voice.

I rubbed my gummy palms on my hips and glanced around. Just
inside the doorway was a clutter of tools we'd left when we
knocked off the day before. One of them was a blocky-headed
maul.

Brandt was still going dok dok on the wall, with his back to me.
I hunkered down and reached and very gently picked up the
heavy hammer. I knew what I was going to do . . . .

I took a deep breath and started toward him, toeing-in like a
creeping Indian. I stared at the back of his head, mesmerizing
myself as I came closer and closer, and his head seemed to expand like a swelling balloon.

Something went squelch in the muck under my foot. I froze.
Brandt raised his head . . . .

By the same author

THE RED FATHOM

Thieves Like Us

ROBERT EDMOND ALTER

Thieves Like Us

WILDSIDE PRESS

PART 1

> "Thus I, together with other thieves who
> are with me, have continued to this day in
> the practice of robbing the tombs of
> Thebes. And a large number of people of
> the land rob them as well, and are as good
> as partners of ours."
> —From the confession of Amenpnu-
> fer, a tomb robber of the Twentieth
> Dynasty . . . 1200–1090 B.C.

· 1

IT WAS almost noon when the guard came in with his jan-
gle of keys. I was sitting on the dirt floor of a vermin-
haunted cell telling off-colored stories to an Arab arsonist
and a Copt dragoman who had attempted to rape an
American schoolteacher inside Cheops' pyramid.

The guard grinned and waited until I had made my
punchline. Then he said, "Come along, effendi. Some fool
is turning you loose on the land again."

I didn't get it, but I wasn't going to sit there and try to
figure it out. So I said goodby to the arsonist and the rap-
ist and they seemed sorry to see me go. I think the guard
felt the same way. He was half bombed on hashish most
of the time and he was a pretty good guy. He got a big
charge out of my stories too, especially the weary old lim-
ericks like: "There was a young man from Dundee, who
buggered an ape in a tree." And so on.

7

"Such rhythm!" he would say. "Such a bubbling flow of words."

He took me to a private office, made a sloppy salute at the Arabian police chief who was sitting toadlike behind a paper-messy desk, and went away. Then there was just myself and the chief and the girl in the room.

I had seen the chief before so I didn't pay any attention to him. The girl was something else. She was blonde and her hair looked soft and silky. Her eyes were very green, dark green, and they stayed calm and careful when she smiled. She wore bright pink lipstick and her mouth had a sulky look that made me want to mash it for her. I don't mean with my fist.

The toady chief wasn't paying any attention to me either. He was so busy giving his eyes a feed on her face and figure he could hardly behave himself behind his desk. She was wearing one of the popular short skirts and she was a trifle careless about crossing her long legs, and that wasn't helping his dignity a damn bit. I didn't have any to worry about.

"Uh — Mr. Ferris, this is uh — Mrs. Brandt." He said it without fumbling it too badly. "She has graciously paid your fine and you are free to go."

That got my eyes off her legs.

"What fine? I haven't been tried yet."

He waved me off with a stubby, impatient hand.

"That has all been taken care of. You need not concern yourself. You are free to go."

Right then is when I should have turned around and gone back to my buggy cell, if I had had any sense. But I was as short on sense as I was on dignity. This Mrs. Brandt — God knows why — had oiled the chief with a little payola. He was dropping the charges against me, and now he wanted me to shut up about it and get out of there because he didn't need the embarrassment. He was a pretty good guy, too. He sold the hashish to the guard and the prisoners.

Mrs. Brandt stood up and gave her skirt a quick practiced brush on the hips, and said, "Well, if there's nothing else . . ."

"Uh — just one thing, Ferris *effendi*," the chief said. "A word of advice. It might be wise if you left Lower Egypt in the very near future. The Department of Antiquities in

8

Cairo might possibly adopt a troublesome attitude about this trifling affair."

"I got you," I said. "Thanks."

I opened the door for Mrs. Brandt and she smiled up at me, a nice gentle smile, and we walked out into the fierce Egyptian sun.

"Can I give you a lift?" She motioned toward a new dust-filmed Ambassador.

"Where to?"

"Back where I came from. Cairo."

"Didn't you hear the nice policeman? I'm not loved in Cairo."

"That's all right. Neither is my husband. But I don't think either of you will be there very long."

I said nothing. I wet my lips and followed her. It was altogether too tempting, and I couldn't say I minded leaving. The little village we were in was mostly sun-baked sandstone hovels and it looked pretty sick set against the awesome spectacle of the Giza pyramids looming in the east.

The inside of the station wagon was like an oven, and she said, "Put up your window. There's an air conditioner that works sometimes."

We rolled down a level tract that was more sand than road and the air conditioner began to drone, working itself into a near fury before it settled down to a contented whir. I turned to her.

"Look. Don't you think it's about time you stopped being so goddam enigmatical and filled me in on your little game?"

She took her eyes off the road for a moment and flashed them on me like green lights.

"No game, Mr. Ferris. It's all quite simple and innocent. I happened to hear about your plight through a mutual acquaintance in Cairo. And as I don't like to see any archaeologist in trouble with the law, I decided to drive out and see what I could do for you. My husband, you see, is an archaeologist too."

I said, "Is he?" Then I thought about her name. "Do you mean Farley Brandt? Is he your husband?"

"That's right. I see you've heard of him."

"Oh yes. I've heard of him."

9

She glanced at me again and smiled her easy smile, but her eyes retained that look of reserve. Now that I was close up and had time to study her I saw she was not quite as young as she dressed and made up to be. I had an idea she was probably born around the time I was. Thirtyish. It didn't hurt her any.

There were ruts in the road and every time she braked that short skirt of hers would slip up a little higher until finally it showed the tops of her nylons. It didn't seem to bother her, but it was a disaster for my sensory receiver.

"What exactly was the trouble you had with the authorities, Mr. Ferris?"

"A technical misunderstanding, Mrs. Brandt. I was conducting a one-man dig in the mastabas behind Mycerinus' pyramid, and it seems my permit had expired."

"Oh? That isn't quite the way that friendly policeman explained it to me."

She paused, and I said nothing, so she said, "My understanding is the Department of Antiquities had revoked your permit for malpractice, and that you were conducting your dig with the intention of selling artifacts on the black market."

Purely out of habit I felt my pockets for cigarettes.

"Do you have any smokes, Mrs. Brandt? I had to share mine with the boys in the calaboose."

"In my bag."

I opened her purse and found a pack of filtertips. I didn't say anything about the tin of contraceptives I saw in there, but she must have known I would see them. I snapped the purse shut.

"The UAR's little bureaucrats frequently get down on an archaeologist when they have nothing better to do, Mrs. Brandt. I believe your husband can attest to that."

She laughed. It was a light, throaty sound and I liked it.

"What are your plans now?"

"You heard what the man said. I've been advised to leave the area."

"So what do you intend to do?"

I took my eyes off her legs and looked at her face.

"Well, I'll tell you, Mrs. Brandt. For some strange reason, ever since I've met you I've had the feeling that you were going to tell me about that. When you get around to it."

She smiled, watching the road ahead. She drove like a

10

man, holding the wheel firmly in her right hand, her left arm cocked on the door. She also drove good-god fast.

"Well, frankly," she said, "it had crossed my mind that you might be interested in a project Farley, my husband, is working on. Professional archaeologists are rather scarce these days with everyone working to remove the monuments before the Aswan Dam floods them. Are you familiar with the New Empire stele in Akhel Foum Valley?"

"No."

I couldn't figure her. Who did she think she was kidding with the "professional archaeologist" billing? She knew exactly what I was: an American Protestant tomb robber — just like her husband, Farley Brandt. Only maybe he wasn't a Protestant.

"Well, Farley got to studying it last year while we were watching the salvage job they're doing at El Sibu, and he decided that perhaps it wasn't just a stele but a tall pylon that had been mostly buried in drift sand. So — to make a long story short, he did some research and came to the conclusion that the pylon *could* be a marker for Akhnaten's tomb. And last spring he hired a gang of *fellahs* and started to dig out the pylon. Last month they uncovered some stone steps."

"All right," I said. "You've aroused my professional interest. Was there a tomb or not?"

"Yes, there's a tomb. Sixteen steps down they uncovered a sealed door."

"Break it open?"

"Not yet." Her easy smile came and went away. "Farley is very careful about legalities these days. We returned to Cairo to get a concession from the Department of Antiquities. It's taken a bit of time and doing."

"I can understand that. The Cairo Museum and the Government Antiquities Service would probably like to feel that if your husband uncovers any interesting artifacts the state will end up with them, or at least a fair percentage of them. So how has he made out?"

"Very nicely, thank you. They signed the concession ten days ago. We return to Akhel Foum tomorrow."

We drove on into the desert and didn't say anything for a while. I thought about Farley Brandt. He was well known in archaeological circles. He was a freelancer. Had to be. There wasn't a reputable exploration group in the world that would touch him with a ten-foot pole. The

11

rumor was that his methods were shady, and had been for over twenty-five years.

The Mexican government was down on him for smuggling artifacts out of Yucatan, he had been run out of Cambodia for the same reason, and the Greeks threw up their hands in dismay at the mention of his name. But for some reason, he had always soft-pedaled his way through Egypt and the authorities had never been able to tag him with anything. And, just to show them that his heart was in the proper place, two years ago he had uncovered an unknown Second Dynasty tomb near Abydos and handed it intact over to the state.

Farley Brandt had done what I wanted to do. He had made a mint out of archaeology and gotten away with it. Undedicated people like us don't dig for love and knowledge. We dig for profit. The Howard Carters can have the glory.

We were approaching that godawful pile of limestone blocks that the old megalomaniac tyrant Cheops had had stacked up as a monument to his own vanity, and Mrs. Brandt braked and I looked at her nylons again and lost my train of thought. Her garterbelt was black.

"Think of it," she said, slowing the station wagon to a mere glide. "One hundred thousand slaves toiled for twenty years to build that, just to protect one dead pharaoh from the tomb robbers. And when it was all finished his family buried his body somewhere else on the sly. That was the most costly deception the world has ever known."

I knew about Cheops and the big trick his family had pulled on the thieves and I didn't want to waste time talking about lost mummies. Not then.

I said, "Stop the car for a minute."

She turned her head and her still deep-green eyes looked into my excited olive-drab optics, and she stopped the station wagon.

I set her purse on the floormat and shoved over on the seat and put my left arm around her. She touched my cheek and laid her head back on my arm and closed her eyes and half opened her mouth and when I got there her tongue was darting between her teeth like a warm, moist asp.

I went out of my mind then, somewhat. And it didn't matter a damn to me if it happened right there on the car seat at high noon in the 112 degree heat, with that 450-foot monstrosity in limestone hulking over us, just so long

12

as it happened. I started my right hand along the familiar course under her skirt, and her thighs were sweat-damp and as soft and slick as whipped pudding, and —

Then she pushed me back.

"Don't you think you should at least know my first name, Mr. Ferris?"

"All right. What is your first name?"

"Greta."

"That's nice. I like an exotic name."

I started to move in again. Her eyes were open now and they met mine, levelly.

She said, "Let's not."

"Why the sudden stop sign?"

"Because I can't quite picture it happening in the back of the station wagon in broad daylight with a half dozen goggle-eyed dragomen peering in the windows. Can you?"

Putting it that way, I couldn't either. But my poor resistless and sensually worked up libido or id or whatever in hell it's called didn't want to throw in the towel that easily. After all, I had just put in six days in that venereal jail, and before that I had spent two sexless weeks working by myself in those damn mastabas. That's a fairly dry spell for a thirty-year-old bachelor.

And Greta Brandt was the type of female who made me feel like a man tied face down on an active anthill.

"All right, then let's go somewhere. There's some mastabas behind Mycerinus' tomb that nobody —"

She laughed. "They must have had you locked up for quite a while. No, Mr. Ferris, I'm sorry. But mastabas are for old dead people, and I don't feel very dead right now. And neither does your hand."

She started the car and looked at me again, smiling.

"Do you mind awfully? I drive better when I can use my legs for the controls."

I took my hand away and put it in my own lap where it belonged. Then I shoved over on the seat to my side and fished in her purse for another cigarette. I didn't say anything as we gathered speed and rolled past Chephren's ruined stone causeway and the smash-faced Sphinx and turned onto the smooth tarmac of the Giza road.

In a little while we were whamming by the posh villas of Cairenes, each nestled in a shady garden with phallus-

13

like palms standing erectilely around them and backed up by lush green fields which sloped into the sun-glinting irrigation canals.

After a fast mute mile, she said, "Mad?"

"You damn well know it, sister."

She laughed her throaty laugh. "Maybe there will be a better opportunity. Later."

I puffed on my cigarette and watched the smooth sea of sand. It was the color of golden wheat in the noon sun. Like her hair. In a little while we entered Cairo.

2

EL QAHIRA it is called in Arabic — the city named after the planet Mars.

I've never liked it. It's too much of an incongruity, too inconsistent. Apartment skyscrapers loom over a section of luxury hotels and tourist-trap shops; and yet a big maze of Arabic and Coptic buildings still cluster in medieval mosques and palaces in the womb of the capital. For my taste it should be one way or the other. Modern or ancient. Not a conglomeration of the worst of one and the best of the other. It looks out of place set against the Giza pyramids standing alone and forlorn on the western desert.

We crossed the long traffic-busy Al Tahrir Bridge and Greta Brandt turned to me with an incurious look.

"Any place in particular?"

"Any place."

So she let me out on the palm-fringed esplanade beside the Nile. I stooped over and looked through the passenger window at her.

"Thanks a lot. For everything."

She smiled lazily and reached for her purse.

"Here. You're broke, aren't you?"

"Not that broke. Besides — I didn't get the chance to earn it. Remember?"

She didn't get mad, as I had expected her to. She laughed.

"Yes, I remember. But let's call it — on account. Take it, for godsake."

On impulse I almost told her where she could put her money. But I didn't. I said, "No. Thanks just the same." Real gone to hell proud. She shrugged.

"Suit yourself. Oh — we're staying at the Lumiere. If you decide to look us up it might be just as well if you didn't mention what transpired today between us and the Giza police. You know what I mean?"

I said, "Um-hm."

"But remember, David Ferris, we're leaving for Akhel Foum tomorrow. That doesn't give you much time to make up your mind."

"I've already made it up," I said.

The funny thing was, I already had.

I had a few piasters left and I went into the first water-side bistro and bought a pack of cigarettes and ordered a dose of rye that went down me like the business end of a pneumatic drill. Then I paid for a ride to the Muski, which is Cairo's bazaar quarter.

I got out in a narrow squalid street and walked to a dingy little shop with the sign SORDO — DEALER IN ANTIQUES over the door.

The interior looked like Dickens' Old Curiosity Shop done in early Egyptian. Everything from scarabs to statues was sardine-packed in a room twelve by twenty, and Sordo, I noticed, still insisted upon keeping Amenemhet's bronze chest beside Queen Hatshepsut's alabaster bust even though they were chronologically separated by six hundred years of dynastic history.

Safi, Sordo's daughter, was standing behind the counter watching me with a flat expression. She was slim, brown haired, brown eyed, and eighteen. And she was something of a problem — to me.

I had gotten shellacked one night when Sordo had gone to Philae on a curio-buying spree. That was when I was living in his spare room over the shop. And along about midnight Safi had come into my room to join me in a drink. One thing had led to another and before I could say boo the entire situation had deteriorated into my bed, and

15

there I was smashed silly with the teenage daughter of the only true friend I had in Egypt.

That had been a couple or three months ago, and ever since I had sobered up and discovered who was in bed with me I had done my best to avoid Safi. For Sordo's sake. But Safi only seemed to be concerned about her sake. She was too young to understand about a friendship between a man and another man. So she had a mad on for me.

"Well David," she said to me in Spanish — she was only Arabian on her dead mother's side. "So you are out again."

"Yeah. I lucked up." I had trouble meeting her fixed gaze. "Is the old man in?"

She indicated the rear room with her head. I took a few steps and then stopped and cleared my throat and looked back at her. Another thing that worried me is that I had been too drunk that night to take standard procedure precautions.

"Safi — are you all right? What I mean —"

"What's wrong, David?" she said in a glacial voice. "Are you afraid you might end up the father of a coffee-skinned child?"

"For crysake, Safi —"

"David!" It was Sordo's voice from the other room. "Is that *el diablo* himself I hear?"

Safi and I stared at each other for a bleak moment. Then she said, "Don't be afraid, David. I'm not pregnant. You won't have to marry a half-caste girl."

I didn't know what to say. I felt low, as if I had snitched a blind man's pencil cup when I didn't need it and didn't really know why I had wanted to take it.

The bedrock truth is I guess I would have started to run if she had said she was pregnant. It was some atavistic prejudice in me I didn't quite understand or want to admit. I liked a change of color, but I didn't like the idea of marrying out of my own race.

"You had better go to him, David," she said coolly. "He knows you are here."

I shook my head for lack of anything to say, and shoved through a carnelian-strung doorway.

Sordo — it was a hand-me-down name; he wasn't really deaf — was half sprawled on a rump-sprung couch, looking at me with bright expectancy. He looked like Sancho

16

Panza, stubby, bay-windowed and spade-bearded. A little scroll-legged Syrian table with a tumbler, spoon, sugar and a bottle of greenish brown fluid was handy to the couch.

He was in the preliminary stage of an absinthe jag, where the drinker glides through a gentle melancholy fantasia of muted song. Thank God he hadn't had time to reach the kooky point where he thought he was dancing with sexy sloe-eyed women on the summit of the Gebel Yelleq Range.

He really was my friend and I liked him. Thirty years ago when he was young he had wanted to be an archaeologist, but before he could get off the ground the civil war in Spain broke out and he had returned to his homeland to fight the fascists. He wasn't a communist — he was an idealist. The only political belief he held was that fascism was wrong for the world. He had been taken prisoner at the end of the war and he had been treated very badly. He never mentioned that gory segment of his life unless he was half shot on absinthe. Then he would start to mumble about the lead pencils up the nostrils and the burning cigarettes against the penis and the hand in the vice with the pliers plucking out the fingernails one by one.

He wasn't any good for archaeology after that; wasn't much good for anything except the absinthe bottle. Kicked out of his own country, he limped back to Egypt and married an Arab girl and casually degenerated into a black market curio dealer.

That was how I met him. I was at the initial end of the business. I found the artifacts and sold them to the curio dealers who in turned peddled them for fancy prices to the affluent private collectors. We were all in the same boat — collector, curio dealer, and digger. All thieves.

Sordo hauled himself up on one elbow and grinned at me.

"*Sangre de Cristo*, friend. They let you go after all!"

I found a fairly clean bronze cup from the Hyksos Period and sat down and poured myself a spot of absinthe. I never went in for it much because there's a scare legend that it makes you sterile. And what the hell; even bachelors like to leave somebody behind, just to show they have passed through this whacky world. Vanity, vanity, all is vanity!

"That's what I wanted to see you about, Sordo. A female by the name of Brandt came out to Giza and paid

17

off the local law to let me go. She said she had heard about me through a mutual friend."

Sordo was nodding like a piston. He reached for the bottle, but I moved it out of his range.

"Take it easy. I don't want you consorting with Suleiman-bin-Daoud and his twelve-winged harlots just yet. What about this Mrs. Brandt?"

"She came to see me, David. Two days ago. She made a point of engaging me in a confidential conversation, just as though she were a common black-market collector. At first I thought she was a spy sent by the Department. Then I began to realize she wasn't actually looking for illegal artifacts. She was trying to find an archaeologist who dug for the market rather than for the state."

He sat up a little higher and fixed his porcine eyes on the absinthe bottle. I placed it in my lap.

"So?"

"So I played stupid, David. Taking no chances, you see? Until I learned her name. Then I knew she was Farley Brandt's wife. And knowing that you had been placed under arrest, I told her about you, thinking she might be able to help you."

I handed him the bottle and thought for a moment. Something, to paraphrase, was rotten in Egypt. That was what intrigued me about Greta Brandt's offer. Where there is dirt there is often paydirt.

"Have you heard that Brandt has wrangled a concession to make a dig at Akhel Foum?"

Sordo nodded. "I have heard."

I thought as much. There was definitely nothing wrong with his ears when it came to rumors of ancient artifacts.

"And that he thinks it might be the Heretic King's tomb?"

"That too I have heard."

"Well, what do you think? Could it be Akhnaten?"

"It could indeed, David. Many of us believe that General Horemheb and the Priest Ay poisoned Akhnaten to seize the throne for their puppet pharaoh Tutankhamen. And because Akhnaten's heresy had caused great civil strife, Horemheb and Ay — hoping to reunite the people — declared Akhnaten to be a false pharaoh and they declined to bury him in the traditional Valley of the Kings. Exactly where they entombed him has been a mystery for over three thousand years."

18

"Would the tomb be worth anything?"

He grinned at me. "Archaeologically speaking?"

"Come on."

"Yes, it could very well be. Horemheb, Ay and Tut were products of their time and environment. They would believe in a strict adherence to the traditional rites and customs. I imagine they poured a king's ransom into Akhnaten's tomb — wherever it is."

He had forgotten about the absinthe bottle. He was watching me with his shrewd, tired, half-rummy eyes.

"Do you think you can get in on it, David?"

"It looks like it," I said. "But goddam — it has an odor to it somewhere."

"You'll have to be very careful, David. Not only of the authorities, but of Farley Brandt too."

"Yeah. Farley Brandt." But I was thinking about Greta Brandt. Those long pretty nyloned legs. And her mouth.

"I'll need a little cash," I told him. "I'm tap city."

Sordo got up with a wheeze and a groan and wobbled blimpishly across the room and pawed aside a drab old Arabic rug hanging over a wall. He came back with a big roll of bills and peeled off a thick rind of them for me.

"Promise me you'll be careful, David," he said before he handed me the money. "I wouldn't want anything to happen to you."

"Don't worry about it, for godsake. I know what I'm doing."

Yes I did.

3

THE LUMIERE was in the Sharia el Maghribi district and it looked like a fugitive from downtown New York. To make matters worse, there was a large garish movie poster on a nearby wall advertising Taylor and Burton in Arabic script, and at the corner of the shrub-clogged corridor that led to the terrace patio there was a fat red Coca-Cola vending machine.

I don't know. I just can't work up much early Egyptian enthusiasm when I see things like that. They look as anachronous as a juke box would in King Tut's tomb, or a TV antenna on the Bunker Hill Monument.

The terrace patio, where the gabby tourists sat around with their fat-faced wives and their gaggle of stork-legged daughters and got half potted while they showed each other the colored slides they had taken of the pyramids, was designed to look like a Hollywood set of the Garden of Allah. It was too vivid, too lush, too much like brighter-than-life technicolor.

I caught a plover-egg-eyeballed waiter in a *tarboosh* and asked him if the Brandt party was there. Just as he started to show me, I spotted them. Or rather I saw Greta Brandt, sitting at a large table with four other people.

Three of them were men. The fourth was a pretty little thing who looked as if she had recently graduated from Vassar and was still consciously pleased about it. But she had made a mistake by parking herself next to Greta Brandt. A visual comparison of the two women was not flattering to her — she took on the aspect of a cute high-school pompom girl.

I knew which one was Farley Brandt. You couldn't miss him if you had heard about him. He was the burly beefeater type, ruddy from the out-of-doors, a deep burnt color that made his grayish eyes seem pale.

I didn't like his eyes. They reminded me of the eyes of a hunter that were accustomed to staring across great distances. I guess I didn't much like his face either, though I didn't know just why — something still and something watchful in it, even when he crinkled up his brown mustache and grinned.

Playing it strictly by ear, I got the feeling from the way Greta Brandt gave me an incurious look that I wasn't supposed to have met her and made a pass at her earlier that day. I didn't show any recognition. I kept my eyes on Farley Brandt.

"Are you Mr. Brandt?"

"That's right, fella. Help you?"

It had been a long time since anyone had called me "fella" and I didn't particularly like it. I had a tight little

20

feeling that he and I were going to start off on the wrong foot.

"Um-hm," I said. "My name's Dave Ferris, Mr. Brandt."

The wrinkles around Farley Brandt's mouth grew deeper, and though he smiled his pale eyes grew more watchful.

"That supposed to mean something to me that I've forgotten about?"

"No, not especially. But we're in the same business."

Nobody had offered me a chair, so I borrowed an empty one from the next table and wedged in between Brandt and the Vassar girl.

"Do make yourself at home, Mr. Ferris," Greta Brandt said, and I almost said "Thank you, Mrs. Brandt" before I remembered I wasn't supposed to know her.

"I looked you up, Mr. Brandt, because I heard you're going on a dig above Aswan. And I need a job."

"Where did you hear that, fella?"

"It's common knowledge in the thieves' market." I tagged a smile on it.

"You an Egyptologist?"

"No. I've only been in Egypt a couple of years. I worked on a Sumerian dig before that, and a few other things."

"What have you done here in Egypt?"

"Not much, actually. I worked under the UAR Ministry of Culture last year, documenting the monuments at Kuban that can't be salvaged in time."

"Why did you quit?"

"Well, it wasn't quite a case of quitting, Mr. Brandt. The team director had a crazy idea that some Twelfth Dynasty artifacts were missing, and I didn't like the way he said it and one thing led to another."

Farley Brandt laughed and the watchful look went out of his pale-quartz eyes.

"Well, fella, I give you credit for coming to the right man. But not at the right time."

He glanced at the two other men. One was about his own age, early fifties, but built like a little bald egg. The other was a young wiry man with a crewcut and smiling eyes, ironic eyes.

"Contrary to what you might have heard about me in

21

certain circles," Brandt went on to say, "I'm not going into Upper Egypt to rob a tomb. Right, Doc?"

Doc was the little egg-shaped man. He chuckled and wagged his chrome dome at Brandt.

"Now, Farley," he said chidingly. "Now, Farley. You know the Egyptian government trusts you."

For a second Brandt's eyes maintained that curious glassy look, and then they twinkled and his smile grew broader.

"That's right," he said. "That's why they've leashed a couple of watchdogs on my prat. They trust me the way Horemheb trusted his wife Beketaten." He swung back to me.

"You ever hear the story of how Beketaten raised the coin to build her garden pavilion at Thebes, fella?"

"Farley," Greta said. "Remember that we have a budding young female archaeologist with us." She smiled at the Vassar girl.

The pretty young thing turned on a tomato face.

"That's quite all right, Mrs. Brandt," she said sharply. "I learned about the facts of life some time ago."

"I'm sure you did, dear. But do call me Greta, won't you? And I'll call you Anne, may I?"

"Oh please *do* — Greta."

It seemed to me it was about to turn into a cat fight. I picked up my original conversation with Brandt.

"I'm not looking for loot, Mr. Brandt," I lied. "I'm flat and need a job. And I'd like to work for you. I think I could learn a lot from someone with your experience."

There was truth in that. I figured I could learn a hell of a lot about the financial end of archaeology — the rewards — from a thief like him.

He was watching me with that look again; smiling, but —

"You do, eh? Well, never let it be said that Farley Brandt stood in the way of a young fella's education. Sure, I'll take you. You said your name was — Dave? All right, Davy. We're getting out of this firetrap at six a.m. prompt, tomorrow."

"I'll be here. Thanks, Mr. Brandt."

He stalled my rise with a hand like a well-cooked ham.

"Might as well meet some of the gang now, fella. We're just one big happy family. This gorgeous sex symbol on my left is my wife, Greta."

22

"Why don't you have another gin sling, Farley?" Greta said in her mild voice. "Maybe you'll say something even more hilarious than that."

Brandt chuckled. Then he turned to the young girl.

"And on your right is Miss Anne Shelby. Grad student. Ethnology. This is her first jaunt into the field of ancient man. I'm taking her along as secretary. But watch out for her, fella, or she'll steal your bloody heart away."

He beamed at Anne Shelby and she couldn't seem to decide whether to smile back or blush again. She was pretty cute but I didn't care. Something was happening to me under the table. Someone's foot was rubbing up and down my right calf.

I looked across at Greta. Her face was void of expression as her foot continued to work on my leg like a fond pet — up, down, up, down. I wet my lips and started to sweat.

"Doctor Jonas Ferber," Brandt was saying. "Master of philology and First Dynasty traveling-salesmen jokes."

"Now, Farley," Doc said, grinning delightedly. "Now, Farley."

I had heard of him. He was well recognized in his field — the study of the Ancient Egyptian language. And I wondered why he had decided to team up with someone like Farley Brandt.

"A little chuckle never hurt anyone," Brandt said. "That's the whole secret of working in these godforsaken places. Just remember to keep smiling — smile, smile, smile."

For a moment there I thought he was going to start singing "Pack up Your Troubles in Your Old Kit Bag." Evidently he was far more loaded than I had realized.

"And last, but far from bloody least, Jeffrey Wren. A free-lance photographer who used to take girly pictures for *Playboy* until he started to branch out into pure pornography and got caught at it."

Jeffrey Wren was the young man with the crewcut and the ironic eyes. He winked at me and said, "Just make it Jeff, Dave."

Greta's foot left my leg and she leaned over to slip on her highheel under the table. Then she stood up, giving her skirt a quick brushdown.

"Excuse me a minute," she said.

23

Brandt grinned at her. "Don't get the wrong one, sweet-heart. They probably have Ladies written in Arabic."

She stopped and looked back and smiled at her hus-band.

"There," she said. "I knew you would be able to top your bathroom humor if you really worked at it, Farley."

We all watched her go away. Her action, viewed from that standpoint, had a beautiful well-rounded flow to it. She disappeared among the potted plants and I let out my breath and stopped sweating. But my leg still felt as if ants were crawling on it.

Then I realized that Jeff Wren was watching me with that goddam ironical look of his. And for a second I thought he winked at me again. But I couldn't be sure.

"Well —" I stood up. "It's been nice meeting you all. I'd better get along. Got some gear to get together. Thanks again, Mr. Brandt."

He leaned back in his chair and the wrinkles in his red face curved into an exaggerated grin as he looked up at me.

"Why don't you give that Mister a rest, fella? Call me Farley. Don't make me feel my sinful years."

"Right. Night everyone." I started away.

"Hey, fella. Need any money?"

"No. Thanks anyhow, Farley. I'm all right."

I wouldn't have taken it from him even if I had needed it. Not when I was going after his wife in the same night.

She hadn't gone to the little girls' room of course. She was standing among the shadowy palm fronds at the rear entrance of the terrace, waiting for me. I stepped into the shadows with her.

"You handled that very well, David. You seem quite proficient at this type of thing. I suspect I'm not the first man's wife you've seduced."

"Yeah," I muttered. I didn't want to talk. I wrapped my arms around her waist and pulled her in tight. She slid her arms around my neck and closed her eyes and opened her mouth and sagged against me, and when we kissed her body began to make a slow hard grind at the groin and that was all I needed to set me off like a satyr on a sex spree. But I didn't get it off the ground. She pushed me back again.

24

"David, David," she murmured. "You do seem to pick the damnedest places to commit a carnal act. A car seat, a mastaba, and now standing against a wall. I'm not an English girl, you know. Standing up doesn't make it any less immoral than the horizontal position to my mind."

"That's a World War Two granny tale," I said. "Not all the English girls think that way. Just some of the cockney girls."

"Well, cockney I'm not. If you know what I mean."

"I'll tell you the truth, Greta. I don't know what you are."

"What's that supposed to mean?"

"That you've got me coming and going. And either you decide that I'm coming — if you know what I mean — or believe me, sweetheart, I'm going. This tease routine you've been playing isn't good for either my organs or my mentality."

She laughed her soft throaty laugh.

"Don't be so impulsive, darling. There will be time. A great deal of time."

Could be. But right then I felt like a misfire at Cape Kennedy. I wanted to go off, I was supposed to go off, but I couldn't get off because some idiot was pushing the wrong timing button, and so I was just a big impotent fizzle.

"Tomorrow night, darling." She put her warm moist lips on mine and mumbled the last two words in my mouth. "In Luxor."

Then, before I could get another clutch on her, she slipped out of my arms, took a quick left turn around a potted palm and was gone. I stared at the dark blank wall and said old dirty Anglo-Saxon words to myself. They didn't help much.

When I turned around Jeff Wren was standing in the blue-shadowed passageway smiling at me.

I went over and pistoled a forefinger in his narrow chest.

"Having a good time, Jeff?"

"I always have a good time, Dave. With or without my cameras. I've learned to take Farley's advice. Smile, smile, smile."

"Well, wipe it off, buster."

25

He didn't. He said, "Speaking of wiping — that's a stunning shade of blushing pink you have smeared all over your mouth. Does it taste as good as it looks on Greta?"

"Look, son of a bitch," I started to say. But I was too keyed up for talk. I decided to show him instead. I led with my left as I was supposed to do, but he tied it up with his cocked right quicker than scat, and in the same instant his left flashed up to my jaw and he tapped me on the chin with his forefinger. Cute.

"That could have been a fist, buddy boy," he said.

I knew it, and that only made me come completely unstitched. I threw my right at his gut, but he swiveled on me and took it on his hip and rolled right back and planted a deep one where I kept my navel, and for the next minute I must have looked like a humped-over monkey making love to a basketball.

He could have done wonders to my jaw formation right then if he had wanted to, but he didn't. He got me by the elbow and helped me straighten up.

"You all right, Dave?"

I had to laugh when I got my breath back.

"I started to warn you that I was a lumberjack once."

He chuckled. "I was about to tell you I was lightweight champ at UCLA. But you were too quick for me."

"My ass, quick. Look, Jeff. About what you saw just before Mrs. Brandt got away."

"Greta?" He looked blank. "She went to the john, didn't she? I haven't seen her. I was looking for you."

I grinned at him. "Thanks. What was it you wanted to see me about?"

"Well, to tell you the truth, Dave, I thought you might want to take a run down to the *dahabiyehs* with me tonight. Last chance, you know. Once we get up to Akhel Foum about all we'll find is a few Copt goat girls. And they tend to be rather dusty and gamy and smell of buttermilk, you know?"

"You're overlooking their most outstanding virtue," I said. "VD. Remember the old limerick about that sorry young girl from Azores, whose breasts were all covered with sores?"

We stopped a cab, and just before we got in, I said, "Look, Jeff. I really am sorry about that punch I tried to throw. As a rule I don't go off the deep end like that."

"That's okay, Dave. I understand. She put me through

26

the same wringer last year when I first met her at El
Sibu."

I didn't know what to say to that.

The streets were crowded as we swung into the Sharia
el Kamel, but our Copt driver knew where he was going
and in a little while he had us out of the business and
pleasure district and took us down a shaded quiet alley toward the Nile. On the Cairo side of the river, just below
where the Kasr-el-Nil bridge links the city to Gezira Island, there is a cluster of ornate *dahabiyehs* — the great
sailing barges of the Nile — moored semi-permanently
just off shore in the coffee-colored stream.

The painted barges, swinging placidly on their hawsers,
were old but not nearly as old as the profession followed
by the females who lived in them. Together, barges and
females, they filled a need that was as old as mankind.
And after the hurdles Greta Brandt had put me over that
day my need was very great.

We went down to a small quay and Jeff spent a couple
of minutes arguing with a gang of Arab pimps. He made a
deal with one of them and we got into a flimsy ornamental
boat and shoved off. Down below us was the Island of
Roda, where legend says the pharaoh's daughter found little Moses in the bulrushes. I wondered if Moses had ever
visited a *dahabiyeh* in his youth.

We pulled alongside a fat squat barge in the dark, and
Jeff said, "I arranged for a pair of sisters. Turkish girls.
Ever tried one? They are something else."

They were indeed. The one I landed was a hot dark
lazy-eyed girl of maybe twenty, and she felt as ripe as a
plump purple plum in the sun, warm and syrupy and soft-
bellied and jelly-breasted, and when I closed my eyes I
told myself it was Greta Brandt and once I even forgot
and muttered her name. But the Turkish girl didn't know
what I was talking about.

4

WE MET the Brandts and Anne Shelby and Doc behind
the hotel. The station wagon was there, the back loaded to
the ceiling, and a Land Rover and a Ford pickup truck,
both bulging with equipment.

Farley Brandt had probably tied one on the night before
but he didn't show it. Compared to Jeff and me he looked
like an eager phys-ed instructor ready to put his students
through their paces. My mouth tasted like a track-runner's
shoe and my stomach was hollow sick. Jeff was swallowing
5mg. amphetamine pills like gumdrops and he gave me a
couple and after a while they began to help.

Greta gave me an incurious look and I looked somewhere else. It was stupid, I suppose, but I felt something
like a twelve-year-old who was caught mishandling himself
in the bathtub. And the pity was, the all-night session with
the blowzy Turkish girl hadn't really helped.

"Ready for it, chaps?" Brandt said to us.

He was wearing boots, riding pants, a corduroy jacket
and a beret. I thought he looked absurd. Two newcomers
were standing by Greta with the mutely ostracized look of
a pair of party-crashers. Brandt gave them a sort of malicious grin.

"Oh-ho," he said. "Almost forgot my manners. This is
Hassan Bey, an inspector of Antiquities from the government." He tipped me a stage wink. "He's coming along to
keep an eye out for thieves. Dave Ferris, O Bey."

"Yes," Hassan Bey said, "I've heard of Mr. Ferris."

He had a slim, erect figure and his high cheekbones,
thin nose and beaklike upper lip gave him the look of an
aristocratic Frenchman. I didn't think he was all Arab or
Copt. He reminded me of a young Zachary Scott.

The other man was Graham Cobb and he was from the
Survey Department. He was lanky and had a sunburned
nose and a soiled white suit. He seemed pretty sour about

the whole thing. Brandt rubbed his hands together energetically.

"Well, boys and girls, shall we be off to see what ancient wonders we can uncover? Jeff, you take Cobb with you in the pickup. Dave, you tail me in the Land Rover with Anne and Hassan. We'll take the Giza road. I'll lead off."

Doc opened the station wagon door for Greta and she paused to glance back at me. I put a cigarette in my mouth and had trouble with the match. Those damn amphetamine pills were starting to give me a ring-a-ding sensation in my hands, like a swarm of bees buzzing under my skin.

"You mind driving?" I asked Hassan Bey. "I feel pretty wrung out this morning."

"Certainly."

"Dissipating, Mr. Ferris?" Anne Shelby asked archly.

"Yes, Miss Shelby. With two Turkish sisters and a bottle of arrack on the Nile."

"Really? I hope you will spare us the sordid details."

"I suppose I might as well, because you already know the facts of life. You said so."

"Coming, Mr. Ferris?" Hassan Bey said in a polite voice.

"Yes, last night."

"Oh *really!*" Anne Shelby was disgusted. I don't think she liked me much.

She got up front with the government thief-catcher, and I climbed into the backseat with a big box of surveying instruments. Then we were on our way.

The big station wagon was booming on down the road ahead of us, and I saw that Hassan had to maintain an average of seventy to keep up with it. Jeff and Cobb were far behind us.

Most of the way to Luxor we drove a blacktop road with dust devils whirling across it like dancing motes of gold. That road is like a luscious party girl all spruced up and waiting for a telephone call that never comes. For hours it meanders along the winding river past small vibrant green fields and dark patches where the soil has been tilled, and through occasional mud-brick villages, and there are white egrets and water buffalo, and more of the

29

phallus-headed date palms, and every few miles you see three- and four-thousand-year-old monuments.

At Sakkara, Hassan motioned toward a giant stone stairway that went up one side and came right down the other.

"The famous Step Pyramid, Miss Shelby. Built by Djoser in 2650 BC. It's the oldest free-standing stone structure in the world."

"It's beautiful. Simply beautiful!" She was breathless about it.

Eight minutes later, at Dahshur, he said, "There's Snefru's Bent Pyramid. About 2600 BC. It's so called because of its blunted shape which was caused by a decrease in the angle of ascent up the sides."

"Wonderful!"

"The ruins of Memphis are across the river. You can't see them from here. But there's really not much left to see."

He was inclined to be a little pedantic, I thought, but I gave him credit for knowing his business even if he did sound like a Copt dragoman conducting a guided tour. Maybe he was trying to make a hit with Anne Shelby. A couple of times when she was goggling out the window I noticed him glance at her lap, and I wondered if she showed as much leg as Greta Brandt did when she was in a car. I leaned forward to talk to him.

"I take it you were one of the stipulations the Department made before they gave Brandt the concession to dig, huh?"

"It's a customary precaution these days."

"Sure it is. Especially when it's someone like Brandt."

Anne turned halfway in her seat to give me a challenging look.

"Exactly what is it that everyone keeps dropping sly little hints about — I mean about Mr. Brandt?"

I said, "I thought you knew the facts of life."

"I'm talking about Mr. Brandt."

"So am I. He's a tomb robber of the first water."

"That's a lie!"

"Ask the government inspector of Antiquities."

She turned her defiant look on Hassan. He continued to watch the oncoming road, but he knew she was waiting.

"Actually," he said, "we don't have a thing on record

against Farley Brandt. All we know is what we've heard from other countries and various exploration groups."

"You see?" Anne Shelby said to me. "It's nothing but malicious rumor. They're jealous of him because he's been able to do so much in the field on his own, without government backing or any society to help him. Why, he's the politest and best-natured man I've ever met. And highly intelligent. He knows more about —"

"And he's married."

She sat straight up and her eyes were as hot as a forest fire.

"You're a horrid beast! An ungrateful, jealous —"

"Amenemhet's temple maze is over there on your right," Hassan said "Twelfth Dynasty. The early Greek tourists compared its puzzle passages to Crete's Labyrinth."

She gawked at him, her mouth still open for business but with the flood of furious words checked. Then she shut it with a snap and turned forward in her seat and glared out the window. She couldn't see the ruins. Hassan hadn't mentioned that they were fifteen miles away.

He was a pretty sharp customer. I started to warm up to him about then.

We stopped for lunch at Asyut, the trade and industrial center of Upper Egypt. Brandt parked the station wagon before a fly-bothered bistro that would have given a Greek frycook the willies, and walked back to us.

"Ready for the feedbag, chaps?" he said boisterously. "Think I'll take mine in the form of a gin snack." He winked at me. "Papa feels a little hung today."

We got out and tramped into the beanery. I tried to catch Greta's eye but she didn't pay me any more attention than she would a Copt barber in a dirty *galabia*. I shared a table with Doc Ferber. On his advice we had hardboiled eggs and dry toast. Even an Egyptian short-order cook can't do too much damage to a combination like that. And I drank three cups of black coffee.

"How you getting on with Hassan Bey?"

"He's a cool one," I said. "Sharp boy."

"He is that, David. He is that. He's caught more tomb robbers in the last five years than the necropolis guards caught in the one hundred and forty-five years of the Twenty-first Dynasty."

31

"That must make Papa Farley feel uncomfortable."

"Speak for yourself, John Alden."

I grinned at him. "What made a man with your qualifications tie up with Brandt, Doc?"

"Same reason you and Jeff Wren and young Miss Shelby did. The days of Egyptian digs being financed by men of wealth are long gone. They belong to the prewar period. Exploration and excavation costs are too steep today for scholars to rely on wealthy patrons. The best one can do is to depend on state subsidies, when you can find one. Or you team up with someone like Farley Brandt."

"And look the other way once he reaches the burial chamber."

Doc chuckled. "Now, David. Farley isn't so bad. His reputation is worse than his bite. Look how he turned that Abydos tomb over to the government, intact."

"Sure. Full of alabaster nothing and bronze worthless. No gold, no jewels. Very big hearted."

Doc was toying with the spoon in his coffee.

"You don't think too much of Farley, do you?"

"I've never been too crazy about beefy bully boys who swagger around with their hairy chests out, yelling, 'Follow me, men.' "

Doc smiled. "Yes, I suppose there is a streak of 'Hail the Conquering Hero' in Farley. A sort of Caesar complex. But Greta, now, is something quite different. Sort of the Cleopatra type, wouldn't you say?"

"Cleopatra was a Macedonian whore, Doc."

He wasn't looking at me. He was staring at his coffee cup, still smiling, faintly.

"Yes," he said, "I know."

We drove on into Upper Egypt and the situation between Anne Shelby and me remained statically cool. Hassan continued to point out and comment on the ancient wonders, and she continued to be impressed.

We passed the predynastic Tasian site, and the ancient city of Thinis, and then the royal tombs at Abydos where Egypt's big poobah god, Osiris, was supposedly interred. I had seen it all before and I really didn't give a damn. The coffee I had guzzled in Asyut had reactivated the amphetamine in my system and I was starting to feel as virile as Bomba the Jungle Boy with his first Watusi maiden.

I couldn't get Greta Brandt off my mind. Or what she had said to me in Cairo . . .

Tomorrow night, darling. In Luxor.

I hunched forward in my seat to speak to Hassan.

"Can't you goose this crate a little? Brandt's going to beat you to Luxor by half an hour."

"Relax, Ferris. We'll get there sooner or later."

Later I didn't care about. But I sat back and kept mum.

The road petered out at El Waqf and we had to ferry across the Nile to Dishna. Then we went slamming on down the east bank to Luxor. It was four p.m.

5

LUXOR is an incongruity like Cairo, only on a much smaller scale. A few thousand years ago it was called Thebes and it was the capital of Egypt. Today a clutter of ancient ruins peg the riverside, surrounded by a swarm of modern buildings. It almost looks as if the 20th-century town means to push the thirty-five-hundred-year-old temples into the Nile.

Luxor got a big play from the rich tourists back in the 1920's when Howard Carter discovered King Tut's tomb across the river in the Valley of the Kings. But, as Doc had said, those days were long gone. Today you see an occasional American dentist and his family, or an English barrister and his secretary, and maybe even a fat pasha from Cairo who is doggedly looking for an American wife.

And Thotmes, Amenhotep, Akhnaten, Tutankhamen, Horemheb and the great Ramesses once ruled the world's first civilization from this place.

It's sad.

Farley Brandt was parked in front of one of the vast, half-empty hotels by the riverside, waiting for us. We

33

pulled in behind him. His mouth was going full blast as he walked toward us.

"All right, boys and girls. In you go. Doc, see about the reservations, will you? Just leave everything out here to me. Papa will take care of the bloody details."

He began shouting directions at a line of Copt porters in a mixture of English and Arabic, making it obvious that we were in the hands of a man who damn well knew the ropes and who knew how to arrange everything in a way that was breezy and bullying and goodnatured. Smile, smile, smile.

Anne Shelby looked after him admiringly.

"Isn't he wonderful?"

"He's a very efficient man," Hassan said carefully.

I said nothing. I went into the hotel to catch up with Greta. She had already started up the staircase with a Nubian bellhop. Doc was heading for the bar, so I didn't have to worry about him.

"Mrs. Brandt," I called. "Just a minute please."

She told the bellhop to go on, and when he didn't understand that, she made a shooting gesture at him and he grinned a pearly grin and went on up to the landing. She turned to me.

"Yes, Mr. Ferris?"

"Stop it, will you? This is Luxor."

"So should I lie down and pull up my skirt here on the stairs?"

"Greta. I just want to know where and when I can meet you."

She glanced over my shoulder. "Farley's coming. The Amenophis temple tonight at eight. He'll be drinking."

I watched her go on up after the bellhop. Then I wet my lips and returned to the foyer. Jeff Wren and the sour-faced Graham Cobb had arrived. Jeff looked pretty well jagged on the pep pills. He grinned at me and pointed toward the bar.

"Time to taper off on some beer."

I nodded and started to follow, glancing at Cobb to see if he was coming with us. He was looking up at the stairs, watching Greta.

"A very interesting bit of female."

His voice was low and harsh and it was the first time I had heard him open his mouth. He hadn't even said how are you or go to hell when we were introduced that morning. I had come to think of him as the quiet little man who wasn't there. Now he suddenly opened up and caught me off guard.

"Who? Brandt's wife?"

"Yes. The *femme fatale*."

"Why do you call her that?"

"Do you need three guesses?"

He brushed by me as if I wasn't really there and he had been talking to himself, and walked toward the desk. I stared after him. Then Brandt and Hassan came in.

"What's wrong, fella? Can't find your way to the gin? Just follow Papa."

I followed Papa into the bar. Hassan didn't come with us.

Doc and Jeff were at a table. They were the only customers in the big barnlike room. A tall Sudanese waiter in a white *galabia* and red sash glided among the wicker chairs to take our orders. I followed Jeff's advice and had beer.

Brandt raised his gin and tonic to us.

"Smile, boys, that's the style."

I suppose he meant it as a toast.

"What's with this Cobb?" I asked. "Does he suck lemons for breakfast or what?"

"Never met the fella till yesterday," Brandt said. He smacked his lips over his gin. "Hassan brought him around to the hotel and introduced him. Said the Department thought it would be just as well to have a man survey the tomb while they still have a chance — before that bloody Aswan Dam floods the whole joint."

"Yeah," Jeff said, "and if you believe that, you'll believe anything. I'll bet my pro kit Cobb's another Department spy."

"Shouldn't be surprised, fella, shouldn't be at all surprised. He have much to say today on the drive here?"

"About as much as the Sphinx." Jeff grinned at Brandt. "The only subject that seemed to interest him at all was your wife, Farley. He didn't break into song or anything like that, but he did ask me a few questions about her. Maybe he's got a secret crush on Greta, huh?"

Brandt laughed. "The young and old, the smart and simple. Greta gets to 'em all." He turned his watchful smile on me. "Can I pick 'em, fella, or not?"

"That's right, Farley," I said. "You can pick 'em."

I wanted to kick him.

"Next thing I know," he said, "old Doc here will be putting on a toupee and slipping up to her room on the sly. Eh, Doc?"

"Now, Farley."

Brandt laughed again. "Who's in favor of another round here, besides me? What's the use of worrying? It never was worth while."

There. I figured he would finally get around to singing 'Pack up Your Troubles in Your Old Kit Bag.'

"Hey, boy!" Brandt yelled at the waiter. "Let's see some service in this direction."

It was well after seven before I could slip away. By then Brandt was telling dirty stories to an American proctologist and a Belgian duke and a *grande dame* from England who used "bloody bastard" in nearly every sentence.

I trotted along the esplanade and then cut over to the Avenue of Sphinxes which once led from Amenophis' temple to Karnak, two miles away. The House of Death used to be somewhere around there and it had been one weird place. That was where they embalmed the bodies. They would use a gimmick like a crochet hook and draw the corpse's brains out through his nostrils, and with another metal hook drag his entire viscera out through his anal aperture. Next they would cut out his heart and replace it with a stone scarab, and then they would take what was left of the poor bastard's body and wash it and soak it for more than a month in a brine bath of salt and lye. Finally the pickled cadaver was hung out to dry for seventy days.

And the funny thing is, none of this ever did the cadaver any good. It wasn't the traditional embalming process that preserved the mummies — it was simply the hot dry Egyptian air and the bacteria-free sands they were buried in that did the trick.

But it was those ancient embalmers themselves who were weird. They ate, slept, lived, hardly ever came out of the House of Death. And when they did they brought with them a smell that was as high as a steeple and nobody would have anything to do with them. Not even the most diseased old harlot would give them a tumble. But they had a way of assuaging their craving for sex. When the body of a young woman — pretty or otherwise — was brought to the House of Death, they didn't go to work on her with their hooks right away. Not for the first night. They cast lots for her, and some lucky corpse washer toted her off to bed. The next day they dumped her in the brine bath.

I don't know. But the guy who said it takes all kinds to make a world had a mighty profound thought going.

I walked into the shadows of the great colonnade that Amenophis III had built fourteen centuries before Christ, and lit a cigarette.

She was standing in there waiting for me, and the next thing I knew she was right beside me. She plucked the cigarette out of my hand and tossed it away.

"Dave —"

And then we were all wrapped up, standing there among the dark towering columns and the old blank-faced statues, and her tongue was going again and she hissed in my mouth.

"Tear me! Tear me!"

I tore her. Blouse, bra, panties, everything. I think I could have gone through steel plating with my bare hands right then.

It was ten o'clock when I got back to the hotel. We were afraid Brandt might be making a night of it in the bar so we had split up at the temple to come back at different times from different directions. I slipped in through the rear entrance and went up the service stairs.

The upper hall was deserted and there was a single weak-watt bulb in the ceiling which was doing about as much good as a match in the middle of the Grand Canyon at midnight. I had almost made it to my room when I heard glass crash. Then the door two down from mine flew open with a bang and Graham Cobb came lurching into the hall.

Lurching was the word for it. His legs couldn't seem to get together about which way they should take him and they had him going from right to left. He had one arm suspended straight out in front of him as if trying to show the rubbery legs the right direction, and his other hand was clutching at his collar as he came bumbling toward me like some kind of nut busting out of a padded cell.

37

And he was making *gaagh gaagh* noises at me in his throat.

All at once his legs gave up and crumpled and he went down like a sack of bricks. He sprawled on the floor and his left leg jerked a little while his outflung hand dug at the mangy carpet. I hunkered next to him and shook his shoulder.

"Cobb. What is it, Cobb?"

His head rolled on the carpet and his face was turning deep purple.

"Hey! Somebody help! Man hurt!"

Anne Shelby was the first to answer. She opened her door and stood there all big-eyed in a skimpy nylon nightie and put a hand to her mouth.

"Oh! What's happened?"

"It's Cobb. He's having a convulsion. Find a doctor."

She started to turn back into her room, and I yelled at her.

"Not in there, for godsake!"

"Well, I can't go like *this!*"

I said, "Jesus," and stood up. Just then Hassan and Doc appeared in the hall. Hassan was wearing pajamas, and Doc was in his shorts and holding a toothbrush. He looked like a startled clown. They both hunched over Cobb and Hassan shook his head and started to get up.

"Looks like he's having a heart attack. I'll fetch someone."

"Don't be in a hurry." Doc spoke without looking up. "He's gone."

I heard Anne Shelby say Oh again, and when I looked around she was back in her doorway wearing a robe. She was staring at Cobb as though she were mesmerized. I went over and got her by the shoulders and pushed her into her room and half closed the door.

"It's no good staring at him, unless you want bad dreams tonight."

"Oh don't try to be so damn flippant all the time!"

"I'm not being flippant. Not about a man's death. I saw a *fellah* crushed to death in a brick cave-in at Kuban. I still see his face at night.'

She bit at her lower lip and stared at the rug.

"I'm sorry," she said in a low key. "The way you usually talk, I thought you were trying to be —"

"I wasn't. I'm sorry I might have said anything today to bug you. It was just one of those days for me."

She nodded, glancing up at me like a shy little girl.

"I'm sorry too — about those things I called you in the car."

"That's all right. You just about pegged me. I guess I am a little jealous of Brandt." That, God knows, was the truth. I put out a hand. "Kiss and make up?"

She looked startled before she saw my hand. Then she smiled and slipped hers in mine and we shook.

"Friends now?"

"Yes, Mr. Ferris. Friends."

"Dave," I said. "Take a sleeping pill, a strong one, and pop in bed now."

"Mr. Cobb — is he dead?"

"Doc says so. Don't think about it. Night."

Hassan was back in the hall with Farley Brandt and the American proctologist. Brandt was carrying his gin like a hard-drinking white hunter in a Hemingway short story, but the rectum-inspector was pretty well bombed.

"Les — let's get him into his room and on the bed," he said in a slurry voice. "Can't hurt to move him now."

"What's the use of worrying," Brandt was humming absently under his breath, "it never was worth while." Then he remembered he was supposed to be the leader.

"All right, chaps. Some teamwork here. Doc, take his right arm. Dave, his left. You and me on the legs, Hassan. All set? Up we go then."

We lugged the poor bastard back to his room and laid him out on the bed. Hassan's foot crunched on something and I saw that a glass tumbler had been shattered on the floor. He turned to the bedstand and picked something up.

"Look at this."

It was a small clear plastic vial with a few tiny white tablets in the bottom. The proctologist took it from him and shook a couple of the pills into his palm. He made an earnest attempt to focus his bleary eyes on them and when that didn't work he gave one of them a lick.

"Nitroglycerin," he said.

"I didn't realize Cobb had heart trouble," Hassan said. "He never said a word about it."

"He should have," Brandt said. "It was a mistake for him to make a trip like this in the heat."

The proctologist was rubbing his face. He looked pretty

39

woozy. I think that aside from the booze, he felt a little out of his element. He was used to working on patients from the other end of the anatomy.

"Well," he said, "I guess it's a clear case of coronary. The authorities will have to be notified, of course."

"Sure," Brandt said.

I looked at him. He wasn't really smiling. He was probably wishing the same thing would happen to Hassan Bey.

6

THERE was no inquest. Hassan told me the next day that the proctologist had signed the death certificate and turned the body over to the Luxor authorities. They would notify Cairo and learn what should be done with the remains.

"Was he a close friend of yours?"I asked him.

It was nine a.m. and we were on our way south again. Brandt was whamming on ahead of us like a fire chief on a holiday.

"No," Hassan said, "not actually. I barely knew him. Our jobs were too diversified."

Yes they were, I thought. I believed the same thing Brandt and Jeff did. Graham Cobb had been a Department agent sent under the guise of a surveyor. The Egyptian authorities trusted Farley Brandt only as far as their spies could see him.

We reached Aswan just before noon and stopped for lunch. Greta, as usual, treated me as though I were a part of the not too interesting landscape. Then we drove up to the First Cataract and took a bleak look at that modern-day marvel which is the bane of archaeology: the Aswan High Dam, *Sadd el Aali*.

We all hated it. Anyone who has any interest at all in archaeology — thief or scholar — hates it. When the god-awful marvel is finished it will put 300 miles of Upper Egypt along the Nile under two to three hundred feet of muddy water. That doesn't just mean the hundreds of little mud-baked Nubian villages; it also means the hundreds of priceless temples, statues, pylons, sphinxes and tombs. You name it and the UAR will inundate it. The untold knowledge of man's early history that is doomed to vanish forever under the dam's reservoir is a crying shame.

And the untold treasures too.

"You really can't blame the UAR," Hassan said, staring blankly at the half-built 20th-century colossus. "They have to drown the past in order to preserve the future. Ninety-nine percent of Egypt's twenty-seven million inhabitants live on less than four percent of the land. And every year our population expands by half a million. Just like ants on a stick of candy. The High Dam will increase the amount of land that can be cultivated by one third. It will help solve Egypt's hunger problem."

I wasn't too concerned about Egypt's hunger problem. I usually had one of my own going. It was all that uncovered ancient loot that worried me. The High Dam might be a boon for the Egyptian farmers, but it was going to put thieves like me out of business. And I belonged to a big brotherhood. And most of them were Copts and Arabs.

An hour later Farley Brandt made his first hand signal since we had left Cairo. Hassan turned to the right and we put the Nile to our backs and started up a one-lane rubble road that threatened to crack the springs.

"There's the pass to Akhel Foum."

He indicated a cluster of small drabby hills that looked like a bunch of meatballs on a platter. Anne got all bubbly about it.

"I can't wait to see it! Just think. What if Mr. Brandt is right and it really is Akhnaten's tomb? It will equal Carter's discovery of Tutankhamen's. Akhnaten was such a wonderful pharaoh."

Hassan glanced at her. "You mean because he was the innovator of the idea that there was only one god — the deity he called Aten?"

"Yes. Just think of it. Thirteen centuries before Christ, Akhnaten was preaching that there was only one God and that He had created everything. And that to Aten, all men were equal: slave and pharaoh alike. Such a startling idea

41

had never entered man's head before. No wonder they call him the Heretic King."

"Um," I said. "But he was also a bit of a weirdo."

She turned in her seat and frowned at me.

"Dave. Are you going to be flippant again?"

"No, I'm serious. I grant you that Akhnaten stands out as the first real individual in history. But to my way of thinking he was an incestuous nut."

She sighed resignedly. "All right. And just how was he incestuous?"

"Toward the end of his life he married his own little daughter Ankhsenpaaten, and she had a baby girl by him. Think about it for a minute and you'll realize that poor Ankhsenpaaten then found herself in the kooky position of being the mother of her own sister."

"Oh that isn't true!"

"Sure it is. If Ankhsenpaaten was Akhnaten's daughter, and if she had a daughter by *her* father, it would have to make her child her sister because —"

"I don't mean that. I mean you're making up a salacious story about Akhnaten just to get a rise out of me."

"Ask Hassan. All I know is what I've read."

She turned to him and he smiled as he watched the tricky road.

"The indications are that he is right, Miss Shelby. An inscription was discovered at Hermopolis in 1938 which implies as much."

Anne Shelby hated to admit that one of her idol's feet might have been made of clay.

"Well," she said dubiously, "philologists have misinterpreted inscriptions before. Perhaps —"

"Look," I said. "Consider the known facts. One: we know that Ankhsenpaaten was Akhnaten's daughter. Right?"

"Yes."

"Two: we know that Tutankhamen married Akhnaten's widow. Right?"

"Y-es."

"And three: we know that Akhnaten was Tut's father-in-law. You see? That clinches it. And if you want to make a real inbred crossword puzzle out of it, remember that Tut was also Akhnaten's half-brother. Amenophis was their father but he had Tut out of *his* own daughter, Sit-

Amun, who was also Akhnaten's sister. See where all that brings you out."

Anne turned around and contemplated her folded hands in her lap.

"It's disgusting," she said. "The most disgusting thing I ever heard."

"You mustn't be too hard on the old pharaohs, Miss Shelby," Hassan said. "They were reared to believe that they were special deities who were incapable of wrongdoing. Therefore, any motivation they saw fit to follow was done with honest justification in their minds. It's an old story. What we condemn as wrong today might very well be the accepted norm of a hundred years from now."

We didn't pursue the subject beyond that point. Hassan swung to the left and the Land Rover went jobbity-jobbity through a hot narrow rock-ribbed pass. Then we were in Akhel Foum.

It was a small parched bowl set in the womb of the barren hills. Circular and smooth, it looked as if the thumb of God had run around the edge shaping it with careful precision. About half of the valley was covered with mounds of drift sand. The rest of it was mostly karoo shrub which can grow where a lizard would curl up and die of dehydration.

The shaftlike stairway leading down to the sealed door of the uncovered tomb was set against the eastern hills. Four fierce-looking *ghaffirs* in blue *galabias* and turbans and with rifles slung on their shoulders were lounging around the pit mouth.

"Oh look!" Anne said. "Those must be the guards who have been watching the tomb for Mr. Brandt. They look just like bandits out of the *Arabian Nights,* don't they?"

They did that. They also looked like men who might have decided to break into the tomb while the cat was away, just to see what little portable knickknacks they could cart off to a convenient and ready market. But Hassan put my mind to rest.

"They're government *ghaffirs,*" he said. "The chief inspector of Antiquities at Luxor sent them here as soon as he learned of Brandt's discovery. Good men."

The little tent camp we pulled into sat in the somewhat shaded center of an old acacia grove, and it was domi-

43

nated by a massive canvas marquee. Brandt got out of the Ambassador with a big grin.

"All right, you hungry tomb robbers. There she is! Just trot your little rear ends down there and see what you see. Hey, Tawwab! Where are you, you old grave ghoul? Doc! See if you can find where Yussuf is hiding, for crysake. Let's get these bloody troops out of the sun and find 'em a little gin!"

Anne, Hassan and I trotted our little rear ends over to the guarded entrance of the tomb. The *ghaffirs* started to stop us, but Hassan exchanged a few sharp sentences with them and that was our open sesame. We went down the steep-pitched sixteen stone steps to a small cleared space before the blocked and plastered doorway.

"Look," Hassan said. "The necropolis seal."

"That's good, isn't it?" Anne asked.

"Very good. It means a person of very high standing is interred within."

"Akhnaten?"

"Possibly. What's wrong, Ferris?"

I was taking a closer look at the sealed door. Close to the royal seal was a faint impression of an even older seal. It could mean that there had been two successive openings and reclosings of the entrance, and the necropolis seal was on the reclosed part of the door.

"We may be three thousand years too late," I said. "Our old friends the tomb robbers might have been here before us."

"Oh, I do hope not," Anne said. "It would be simply awful for Mr. Brandt."

"For all of us, Miss Shelby," Hassan reminded her. "The Department of Antiquities is just as interested in this tomb as Farley Brandt." He glanced at me. "From a scholarly viewpoint."

I said nothing. I put a cigarette in my mouth.

He said, "Well, I'd better get back and see when Brandt intends to make the initial opening. Will you both excuse me?"

"He's awfully nice, isn't he?" Anne said after Hassan had climbed the stairs and disappeared into the hard blue glare of sky overhead. "His name doesn't seem to fit him, though. I mean he looks and acts more like a European baron than an Arab policeman."

"Yeah. I have an idea his mother's name was probably

44

O'Hara or Smith. Listen, Anne. Did you know Graham Cobb before Hassan brought him to the hotel the day before yesterday?"

"Mr. Cobb? Why, no. None of us did that I know of. Evidently Mr. Brandt and the others had known Hassan Bey for about a month, but Mr. Cobb was a stranger to them. I think the Department must have made a last minute decision to send him with us."

"Yeah. Why do you say Brandt and the others had known Hassan for a month? Where were you?"

"I? Why I only applied to Mr. Brandt for a job two weeks ago. Why all the questions? Is something bothering you about Mr. Cobb?"

"He's dead, isn't he?"

"Well, of course he's dead. But things like that happen all the time. Heart failure. He must have been in his late forties."

"Um-hm. I'm probably batty, but it's the coincidence of the damn thing that bugs me."

"What coincidence? I don't understand."

I shook my head. "Neither do I. To hell with it. I just get some weird hunches now and then. They usually don't mean a thing. I told you I was batty, didn't I?"

And maybe I was, somewhat. Because right then I wasn't actually thinking about what had happened to Graham Cobb yesterday. I was thinking of something that had happened thirty-three centuries ago.

Horemheb and Ay had wanted to seize the throne of Egypt. But Akhnaten had been sitting on it. So they had put some poison in a cup. . . .

None of us except Brandt did any work for the rest of that day. Papa was out in that Egyptian blast furnace having his gang of *fellahs* — the native workmen — unload and sort out our digging equipment. The rest of us just lazed around in the marquee and drank gin and beer. Greta, Hassan, Anne and Jeff got up a game of bridge, and Doc dozed in a camp chair and sweated like a pig.

I got bored after a while and went out in the heat to talk to Brandt. I asked him if he had noticed that second seal impression on the tomb door, but he just laughed it off.

"Might not mean a thing, fella. Could be the necropolis

45

guards opened it for a spot check. They did that to a lot of tombs in the Twenty-first Dynasty. Checking up on the thieves. Then they would reseal 'em."

"Sure, but it could also mean the guards discovered the tomb had been defiled and they resealed it against a second attempt."

"Don't court disappointment, boy. Why would they bother to reseal it if the thieves had cleaned out the joint? Look what happened at Tut's tomb. The thieves got in there all right, but they were caught before they could grab the loot. So it was resealed, covered over, and forgotten for three thousand years."

He grinned and gave me a hail-good-fellow slap on the back.

"Think positive thoughts, Davy. Always positive thoughts. Smile, boys, that's the style. What's the use of worrying? It never was worth while."

I walked off and left him humming to himself. The only positive thought I had right then was about his wife.

We met that night in a little setback among the meatball hills. It was screened from the camp by karoo bushes. I had brought along a blanket but it didn't do me much good at first. Greta was feeling moody.

"Not yet, Dave. I want to talk to you."

"Talk is for after."

"Not this time. We have to make some kind of decision."

"About what?"

"We can't go on like this, Dave."

"Like what? We haven't done anything yet, except last night."

"You know damn well what I mean. If it were left up to you we would just go on night after night like tonight and last night. Sly little assignations in the sand dunes."

"Well," I said, "I've done worse things with my time."

"It isn't good enough. Not for me. I don't like sneaking. If I love someone, I want to love him in the open. Not like this. And if I have to go on living with Farley much longer I'll start howling at the moon. It's like going to bed with a man who was a burly storm trooper in the last war."

"Why did you marry him? He must have twenty-some years on you."

"Why do you think? Because I admired his manly chest and the way he swaggers around telling everyone what to do? For his money, of course. Five years ago I was working as a model in Paris, when I could find work. When Farley came along and started drooling over me, I took him. Do you blame me?"

"No. How come you were in Paris?"

"I went to the Riviera with my first husband. He was a sweet guy but a worthless bum. A gambler. His luck went sour and he got in over his head, as far in as a man can go. When he learned I was pregnant, something snapped. He shot himself."

"What did you do about the baby?"

"Guess. So then I went to Paris and tried modeling. There's always some fat buyer with a fat wife and four fat children in the background who tries to run his sweaty hand up between your legs on a job like that. And if you want to keep the job and keep on eating, you stand there and take it and pretend you like it and want some more, and then later —"

"All right," I said. "I've heard about it before."

"I'm only telling you because I want you to know I'm being completely honest with you, Dave."

"Yeah, yeah. But I don't want to hear about it. So then what?"

"Then Farley came along. I didn't love him. I didn't really like him. But he wasn't fat and sly and he didn't have a wife and four kids. And he had money."

"That's a big point in his favor."

"Yes. It was at first. Now I'm so sick of him I could puke. Sometimes I think if I see him slap one more person on the back and say 'Smile, fella, that's the style!' I'll go out of my mind."

"Well, I've heard there's such a thing as divorce."

"Not for Farley there isn't. That's part of the storm-trooper act. He likes to keep people under his thumb. Especially when he knows they want out."

"You've asked him?"

"Of course I have. But he laughs at me and knows he can get away with it because I don't have any grounds. And without grounds I'd have to settle for a penny-ante alimony."

47

I started to dig out a cigarette but decided I better not. Somebody might notice the light in the dark.

"Well," I said, "there's another way. You and I could just take off."

"To where?"

"Um — Yucatan, Iran, the Aegean Sea. Anywhere."

"And rob tombs and try to live on the black market? No, David. I was married to one man like you who lived from hand to mouth. Once is enough in any girl's life."

"Farley does all right at it," I reminded her.

"Yes. Now. But it took him nearly fifteen years of living like a sandhog and being chased by the authorities and kicked out of countries before he could begin to make it pay off. I can't live that way, Dave. Look where you were when I found you."

"Um, but you seemed to go for me."

"I did more than go for you, darling. I fell for you. Hard. You're young and clean and strong. You're intelligent, and you don't smell of gin all the time or swagger around like Alexander the Great."

I grinned in the dark. "My God. How much more can you want?"

"Be serious, Dave. It isn't good enough. Without money it isn't nearly good enough. We're not a couple of high-school dropouts who want to get married and go live in a two-room flat in some grubby city. We need the best, and that means money. You wouldn't be in this business if you didn't want money — a lot of it."

"Yes," I admitted. "I did think that way — right up until I met you. Now you're all I really want. Nothing else seems to mean a good goddam to me."

"You'd get over that, though, after a couple of years of living in Greek slums and chasing third-class steamers and eating stale sandwiches in cheap bistros. You'd start to feel the drag. And then you'd begin to look at me as an anchor around your neck. It wouldn't work. You know damn well it wouldn't."

I rubbed at my mouth. I wanted a cigarette and I wanted her, and I knew that basically everything she had said was true, and I felt so christly frustrated I wanted to get up and chase myself in circles.

"Well then what in hell are we supposed to do?"

She was silent for a while. She sat there and stared at the black karoo bushes in front of us.

48

"There is one other way, Dave."

That was when I should have stood up and walked away. Not just away from her and the blanket and the set-back, but out of the camp and Akhel Foum and Upper Egypt. And kept on going. Because right then is when I knew exactly why she had prowled around the thieves' market in Cairo looking for a young, not-too-scrupulous archaeologist, and why she had gone to Giza to bribe the police into releasing me.

But I didn't because I couldn't. Because now it was too late and I was in love with her. And because I told myself that maybe that was all she had wanted me for in the beginning, but that maybe now she had fallen in love with me too.

"They do unpleasant things to people for that sort of business, Greta. The UAR probably uses a firing squad."

"It doesn't really matter what they use, does it? As long as you're not caught."

"And who says we won't be caught?"

"For what? Being present at the time of a tragic accident?"

"An accident —"

"Yes. In a tomb — where the ancient architects rigged deadfalls and pitfalls to catch thieves. It's happened before, darling. And it can happen again — if it's done intelligently."

I wet my lips and said, "It's not quite in my line. I don't like Farley, but this sort of thing . . ."

She slid across my lap and put a hand behind my neck and pulled my head down and started working her eyelashes on my face, making butterfly kisses on my cheek.

"We're wasting the blanket, darling," she whispered.

I rolled her over and got rid of my pants and reached for her again, and she was breathing words.

"It's going to work, isn't it, darling? Tell me, tell me . . ."

For a wild second there it felt as if I were being lowered into a barrel of warm honey, and when she said, "You know it will, don't you, don't you," in my ear, I said, "Yeah, yeah," impatiently, wanting her to shut up, but she didn't, saying, "You'll work something out, won't you, won't you," and me saying, "Don't worry about it for godsake, I'll take care of it," and still she kept at it, pant-

49

ing, "And soon, darling, promise, promise," and I said, "Yes, for crysake, yes, now shut up."

Then she shut up.

7

THE NEXT day we made the initial cut in the tomb door.

Brandt and I did most of the grouting and the *fellahs* scooped up the plaster shards as fast as we could chip them out. Hassan, Doc and Anne stayed up on the top step and watched us. They looked like idle extras in a Jungle Jim film in their pith helmets. Jeff had a 16-mm. camera set on a tripod, and a strap camera around his neck, and he was as busy as the famous one-armed paperhanger with all his little meters and gadgets.

Greta stayed in the marquee by herself and played solitaire. We had decided the night before that it might be just as well if she didn't show too much interest in the tomb. For one thing it would keep us apart during the working hours, and that was wise. When a man and woman are shacking on the sly they usually give out unconscious indications of it around other people — a look, a touch, a too obvious sense of nearness.

Around ten in the morning we had a fair-sized peephole bored in the door, and Brandt inserted an electric torch and took a peek.

"Yeah," he said. "I thought as much. The entry corridor is filled to the brim with rubble."

He straightened up and winked at me.

"Looks good, fella. Looks better all the time."

"Why is that, Mr. Brandt?" Anne called down.

"Well, little girl, it gives me further reassurance that the necropolis priests took elaborate protective measures to seal the tomb against thieves." He clapped a meaty paw on my shoulder.

"Yes sir, I think we've got a live one in here. Hey,

50

Tawwab! Let's see how quick those lazy beggars of yours can crack open this vault."

Tawwab was the foreman of the *fellahs* and he nearly wetted himself like a praised puppy every time Brandt yelled at him. He gave me a big toothy look, as if saying wasn't Brandt *effendim* the grandest man ever?

"Where's Yussuf with the gin, for godsake?" Brandt roared. He pulled a mock punch at my gut. "How about a cold one, fella? Hot as Set's hoof down here."

Big Brother was in high spirits.

We went up and sat down under the umbrella that Brandt's gin-bearer, Yussuf, had set up for us, and Anne and Doc joined us. That fool Jeff hung in there with his cameras under the hammer-and-tongs sun, and Hassan stayed with him.

"Look at that bloody watchdog," Brandt said to us in a low voice. "Scared to death one of the boys will slip a bit of potsherd in his *djellab*."

"Now, Farley," Doc said reprovingly. "That's his job. And they need watching. There's a ready enough market for antiquities downriver, and the temptation to supply it has been known to be too great for the simple Arab conscience before this. As you well know."

Brandt chuckled and reached for his iced gin.

"Doc, Doc. You keep forgetting I'm a reformed character. I'm here in the interest of Egyptology. Not for loot, heaven forbid." He raised his glass to us. "Chin chin."

"Chin chin," Anne said brightly and took a sip of hers.

I wanted to throw up.

Tawwab came up to us in about an hour, bowing like an obsequious mouse, and informed Big Brother that the doorway was now open.

"C'mon, group," Brandt said. "Let's see what the past has to tell us."

It wasn't much. As we already knew, the entrance passage was filled with stone chippings, stacked tight like rip-rap in a retaining wall. But this filling consisted of two kinds of stone, and we could clearly distinguish an old shoulder-wide tunnel in the six-foot wide corridor. This tunnel had been filled with dark shards of flint.

"Oh oh," Brandt said, "trouble ahead." He tapped the oval-shaped fill of flints.

"See this plug, Anne? It means our old pals the tomb robbers burrowed out this little crawlthrough for them-

51

selves. Later on the necropolis guards replugged it with this flint."

"Does that mean we won't find anything inside the tomb?"

"Not necessarily. If they went to all the trouble of replugging and resealing the tomb, there's still a good chance we'll find something of value in there. Just cross your fingers and pray, boys and girls. And smile, smile, smile. That's the style."

Now that we had most of the rubble blocking the bottom of the stairs cleared away, we uncovered potsherds with the names Akhnaten, Smenkhkare and Meritaten on them.

"What the hell?" Brandt said. "What do you make of this, Doc? What are these bloody potsherds doing away out here at the front of the tomb?"

"I really can't say, Farley. And I don't understand why there would be three names."

"It could be an indication that this is a jointly shared tomb," Hassan suggested. "There's no certainty that Smenkhkare's body has ever been found, and I don't believe anyone knows what became of Meritaten."

Brandt beamed at him. "Don't give me hope like that, fella. All I'm asking for is one lost pharaoh. Not two of them *and* a queen."

Hassan smiled and said, "With your permission, I'll have the *ghaffirs* collect these potsherds for cataloguing."

"With *my* permission?" Brandt was grinning at him. "Could I stop you if I wanted to? All right, fella. Just a joke. Sure, get 'em to hell out of here. Tawwab! Let's see some action on this passageway. I want it as clean as a Nubian's heel. Say, who's ready for a snifter in this group? By God, it's hot as hell in this pit, eh?"

That's how it went for the rest of the day. By sunset the boys had penetrated twenty feet into the entrance passage, and still they were faced with a solid wall of riprap. Anne and I walked back to the marquee together.

"Who were Smenkhkare and Meritaten?"

"Smenkhkare was Tut's brother and Akhnaten's half-brother. He married Akhnaten's daughter Meritaten, who was his own niece, and Akhnaten set him up as co-regent for the sake of politics. Then after those two shrewd thieves Horemheb and Ay poisoned Akhnaten, Smenkhkare became a full pharaoh. But Horemheb and Ay couldn't have that, so they arranged an accident for him."

"They killed him?"

My mind had wandered out of the dim past and into the near future. *They arranged an accident for him . . .*

I said, "Huh? Oh — yes. They saw to it that he had a little accident in a boat on the Nile. So Tut became pharaoh."

"Well, I don't see that that got them anywhere. What did they do then — murder Tutankhamen, too?"

"Not then. You see, Horemheb and Ay didn't give a damn about glory. All they wanted was power. And Tut was only eight years old. They made him a puppet pharaoh, but they were the real rulers of Egypt. Then about the time Tut was eighteen, they helped him pass into immortality and Ay grabbed the throne. For a while. Until Horemheb decided it was his turn to be boss."

She shook her head with a wondering look.

"Where do you learn all these things?"

"A lot of it's just supposition. But you read a little here and listen to a little there, and suddenly it all begins to form a pattern. Man's basic drives never change, you know. The desires that motivated men three thousand years ago are the same atavistic cravings that drive most of us today. Glory, power, wealth, sex. We all want something we don't have. Something that usually belongs to somebody else."

"What is it you don't have that you want, Dave?"

"Well," I said, "power doesn't mean a damn thing to me."

The next day the boys uncovered a small chamber cut out of the side of the sloping passage. The niche contained a skull and three legs of an ox and two beer jars. It was a sacrificial offering.

"Match you for the beer, Dave," Jeff said. "Nothing like warm three-thousand-year-old beer."

Warm was a weak word. It was so goddam hot and airless in there we were all wringing wet. It was like swimming in boiled glue. Late in the afternoon the sweating *fellahs* removed the last of the riprap, and we were facing a wall which was inscribed with the little pretzelstick hieroglyphics.

I was never much good at that sort of thing. I can recognize a lot of the glyph symbols on sight, but you have to remember to read each one backwards in order to construct a sensible sentence. Reading them the way the Egyptians inscribed them in either the hieratic or demotic script, you can come up with something like: "I place hands my against breast your."

The dust from the riprap had congealed in the little glyph grooves, and Doc said, "Someone give me something for a pick."

I gave him my pocketknife and he stood on tiptoes and scratched at the intricate glyphs with the point of the knife. In a little while he rocked back on his heels and grunted.

"It's the usual psychological scare for thieves: 'Death shall come on swift wings to those who disturb this tomb.'"

"I wish the bloody thing said 'To those who disturb the rest of the Pharaoh,'" Brandt growled. "Hell, this tomb could belong to any high dignitary — from a common mayor to a general."

"Think positive thoughts," I told him.

His still eyes flashed at me. Then he chuckled.

"That's one for you, fella. You caught Papa off base that time. Well, who's got the chisel? This bloody wall is as false as a thirteen-year-old girl's bra. Let's see what we have on the other side."

He made a small breach in the plastered wall in the upper left-hand corner, humming as he worked, and then took a long iron testing rod and ran it through the hole as far as it would go.

"Darkness and blank space," he said. "How far in have we come, Hassan? Fifty feet?"

"Exactly."

"Good. The shaft to the burial chamber should be right on the other side of this wall then. Gimme the candle, Tawwab."

He inserted a flame-fluttery candle and winked over his shoulder at Anne.

"Precaution against possible noxious gases. Remember that next time you break into a tomb."

The hot air escaping from the inner chamber nearly put out the little peak of flame. Brandt took a look inside and said, "Hell. No shaft. It's a continuation of this descending passage."

He stepped back and blew out the candle and grinned at us.

"Well, boys and girls, I've got a sneaky hunch we're in for one of those old Egyptian puzzles. So let's call it quits for today and get out of here before we all melt into soup. C'mon. Last one to the gin is a Nubian's knocker. What's the use of worrying? It never was worth while."

Greta and I lay on the blanket again that night and stared up at the staggering drift of star sparks. Our clothes were in a dark clump beside us. We were so close I could smell the scent of her hair. It was like the pure essence of Tartary musk.

"You think it has possibilities?"

"Yeah. If Papa is right, it has damn good possibilities. If it was designed as a labyrinth to trick thieves, then we'll likely run into some pitfalls tomorrow."

She let out her breath. "Mrs. David Ferris, wife of the eminent and affluent archaeologist."

"On his wife's money."

"Shut up. Kiss me, David. Here."

I kissed her there.

Ten minutes later she said, "Be careful tomorrow, darling. Be very careful. But when you do it, do it good."

Little David almost did it too good.

PART II

8

BRANDT was right. It was a labyrinth.

We broke through the inner door the next morning, and Papa led the way down the sloping passage with a Coleman lantern. The corridor descended for another fifty feet and suddenly dumped us into a *cul-de-sac* chamber about the size of a dressing room.

The limestone walls rose around us to a height of nine feet, and in the dazzling lantern light we could plainly see the hole the old tomb robbers had cracked through the false ceiling.

"Well," Brandt said, "at least the thieves have saved us a lot of time looking for the next passage. Tawwab! Have the boys fetch in a ladder."

Jeff shooed us all out of the chamber so he could take pictures, and we stood back in the passage like sardines and waited. And sweated. That foul air would have turned a sloth's stomach.

"It's amazing," Anne said, "how those old tomb robbers always seemed to know just where to go once they were inside a tomb."

"Not as amazing as you might think, Miss Shelby," Hassan said. "They usually had advance information, and even diagrams of the tombs; all supplied by bribed priests and corrupt officials. Those gangs of thieves, you see, were highly organized and were recruited from all social levels."

"I think it's deplorable," she said. "Thank God man is more basically honest today than he was three thousand years ago. Even if Dave doesn't agree with me."

Hassan shot a wry glance at Brandt.

"That's debatable, Miss Shelby. Even today archaeological honesty and dishonesty have their degrees. For example: Lord Carnarvon, who was Howard Carter's partner, removed some priceless artifacts from Tutankhamen's tomb to add to his personal collection in England, even though Carter and the Egyptian government claimed he had no right to do so."

"Why that made him nothing short of a thief!"

"Sure," Brandt said to her. "Just like us. Even if he was an English lord."

Two of the coffee-skinned *fellahs* shoved in with the ladder and banked it against the north wall. Doc was explaining some painted friezes to Brandt and Anne, and Hassan was helping Jeff get his gear out of the way. No one was paying any attention to me, so I scrambled up the ladder with a flashlight.

I climbed through the hole and found myself in what would be known as a grand gallery. It was a large horizontal passageway: seven feet wide and twenty feet high, its walls made of polished white limestone and decorated with the inevitable friezes showing the endless procession of Egyptian characters, always in stiff profile, always moving toward some unseen goal.

The only one I recognized was Akhnaten. But he's easy. He is usually depicted with a baywindow and an elongated head. He was the only pharaoh who believed that artists should paint what they saw, not what the pharaoh wanted to see.

About twenty yards on, the passage narrowed down to a small opening that was not quite shoulder width. I leaned into it cautiously and had a look with the flashlight. A thin column stood just inside the doorway and it had not been mortared to the floor. It had all the earmarks of a trigger post, and I saw I was right when I looked overhead. A massive wooden beam, a false lintel, rested on the column over the inner archway.

I drew back and wet my lips. It seemed that the time was now.

"Farley! C'mon up. There's a gallery here."

A few seconds later his ruddy face emerged through the hole and he raised the lantern and looked for me.

"Oh-oh," he said. "I hope you haven't slipped any funerary gems in your pocket while Hassan's back was turned, fella."

I think Big Brother was a little spiffed because I had gone ahead of him and seen the grand gallery before he did. He walked toward me, looking right to left and up, and I waited until he had almost reached me. Hassan was just scrambling through the hole.

"Watch your step," I said to Brandt, and eased myself through the doorway. "It's tricky here."

I stopped just inside the opening with my body covering the trigger post, and flashed my light in his face just as he ducked his head and started to wedge himself through the doorway. His eyes winced shut.

"Hey hey, for godsake, fella!"

"Sorry."

I swung the light away and stepped back as if to give him more room, and I gave the column a good bump with my butt. I felt it give behind me, and there was a crackling overhead as the false lintel started to let go.

Brandt yelled *"Jesus, look out!"* as I took a blind broadjump in the opposite direction. A great load of limestone blocks came crashing down in a dusty shower and for a full minute I couldn't see a thing for the opaque cloud of swirling dust. The thunder of the crash echoed far down the unseen corridors and slowly died out.

"Brandt!" I shouted. "You all right?"

I thought I heard him answer but I wasn't sure. If it was him, then his voice was too muted. Anyhow, the damn dust got me coughing so violently that that was all I could hear for a couple of minutes. When it settled I had a look at the damage with the flash.

It wasn't good. The high ceiling of the inner gallery was formed by overlapping courses of masonry and a whole raft of giant square stones had come down and stacked themselves in front of the opening like building blocks.

I was goddam well sealed in.

58

"Kay-*riced!*"

I didn't know what else to do but stand there like a dunce and swear. Because it was my own fault. Because I should have had enough sense to see if the false lintel was supporting a deadfall of mere riprap or five tons of stone blocks before I triggered the trap. It would take them days to cut through that! And meanwhile I would be sitting in there with dead batteries in my flashlight.

No food, no water, and nothing much to use for air.

I went a little crazy then. I started pounding the stones with the butt of the flashlight but I stopped it when the light began to flutter on and off like a dying man's pulse. Then I heard a *clack clack*. It sounded hollow and far off but at least they knew I was still alive in there.

But could I hold out until they reached me?

I looked at the gleaming flashlight. I don't mind the dark if I think I'm going to get out of it in a reasonable time. But three or four days of it is too much of a stretch. God hadn't rigged my id for solitary confinement.

Come on, smart bastard, don't just stand here with your finger up yourself. Do something!

I started walking toward the far end of the gallery, the flashlight casting weird, wobbly shadows on the bright corbeled walls looming high over me. Along the lower portion of the sidewalls ran a tiered series of square rampstones. They were four feet high and appeared to be a footing for the upper courses of masonry. One of them was standing slightly catawampish to its brothers and looked as if it might be a false stone the necropolis guards had forgotten to set in place the last time they were in the tomb.

I hit it a few spots with the heel of my hand, looking for the pivot point, and found bingo on the fourth try. One end shoved inward, the other swung toward me. I hunkered down and had a look with the flash.

It didn't look like anything a man would be in a hurry to rush into; but then it didn't seem to be any worse than the passages in Cheops' pyramid either. It was almost four feet high by three wide, and the walls, floor and ceiling were made of well-cut limestone blocks.

I could have continued along the grand gallery but I figured that would only take me to another deadend chamber. This secret passage was probably the route the tomb

59

robbers had used. So I decided what the hell, and hunched over like Quasimodo and started into the tunnel.

It wasn't too bad at first, if you're used to crawling around in those rat warrens. But it would be a mighty poor place for a novice to discover he had a tendency toward claustrophobia. I hulked along for about ten feet and then the passage forked on me.

On the right a tunnel sloped upward, going north. The other sloped downward, going south. I took the south bore. If the tomb's architect had followed tradition, then the north bore would go in the direction of the burial chamber, and I didn't want that. What I wanted was to get out of that big spooky sonofabitch.

The limestone siding continued for about thirty feet more, then the construction of the walls began to deteriorate and I was passing through solid bedrock. After that it got worse.

The narrow tunnel led down, down like a slanted shaft leading into Dracula's cellar. The kind of shaft that blood-sucking old bastard might have used for a corpse chute.

I hunched along at a slow pace, watching for pitfalls, the flashlight shining eerily along the bore of naked rock that stretched and descended ahead. If that light petered out I would be a man lost in infinitely abysmal earth, pawing, twisting, panting, scrambling madly through sunken convolutions of immemorial blackness without an idea of time, safety or direction.

It made me feel like a mole burrowing in the blind earth. Or a grub struggling for life in nighted depths where unclean things grew. You can think a lot of kooky thoughts in a place like that. You tell yourself Nuts, but you go on thinking them just the same.

There were changes of direction and of steepness. And once I came to a long low level passage where I had to wriggle like a worm on my gut along the rocky floor, holding the flash at arm's length ahead of me. The godawful place wasn't high enough to even kneel in. Then the passage raised but didn't broaden. I could stand up like a man again. It was a good feeling.

It was a chamber of sorts; ten feet high, but the passageway was still only a yard wide. Both sides of the rock walls were tiered with thick hardwood shelves rising one above the other like bunks in a troopship. I flashed the light to the left and it splashed squarely on a contorted face gawking out of the wall with empty eyesockets.

What I mean — I moved!

I took a blind backward jump on sheer reflex, my spine clobbering the shelves behind me, and something dry and scaly rasped across the back of my neck and started to slide over my shoulder.

I yelled "No!" and lurched to the right, and the christly thing plopped on the floor. I'm not a superstitious person, but there is something of the mystic in every Christian, and when I saw that thing in the halo of light thrown by the flash, my hair seemed to stand on end.

It was an old dried forearm with the scraggly hand and spidery fingers still attached.

My heart was jackhammering, but other than that I was all right. More or less. By then I realized what I had gotten myself into. The passage was choked with mummies — not the kind like Tutankhamen; there were no coffins or wrapping sheets. These sorry bastards had never seen an embalmer. They had been stacked in there bareass naked.

It was the kind of communal sepulcher that the Egyptologist Belzoni had found in Thebes in 1816, where poor people who could not afford individual tombs were buried in gangs, the bodies being stacked from floor to ceiling like bolts of cloth. But what didn't make sense was that the necropolis priests never put a royal seal on a communal grave. So who were all these mummies?

Eyeless, jawless, an arm missing here, a leg gone there, their Halloween faces gawked at me from everywhere. Withered and shrunken, they looked like bundles of old twisted sticks in a dark basement.

I said, "Christ," and started pushing my way through them.

It was like finding yourself in the grotesque world of an Edgar Allan Poe short story. The air was suffocating and many of the old shelves had caved in, forcing me to wade through a horrific mire of broken mummies, which started clouds of dust swirling that got in my throat and nostrils and choked my nose and mouth, and on top of that there was the good-god effluvium of the mummies themselves and that was a real gut-clutcher.

The downward incline of the passage helped some by giving my body weight impetus, but I couldn't seem to

61

keep from putting my sweaty face in contact with some gape-mouthed decayed Egyptian, and the farther I forced myself the more I became covered with bones, legs, arms and even grisly heads rolling from the crumbling tiers above, and it was like trying to wedge through an antediluvian gantlet of gnarled limbs with the brittle old hands clawing at my clothes, ears, hair . . .

Out. Sweet Jesus Christ get me out of here.

I hadn't been consciously religious since I was about ten years old. But now I was and I meant it, and it seemed to me at the moment that I would never mean anything more in my life.

Please Christ, I'll never try to hurt another human being as long as I live but just get me goddam out of here!

The nightmare passage ended. A narrow breakneck flight of rock stairs stepped on down into the warm darkness below me and I followed them without even pausing to wonder where they would take me.

I wasn't more than half crazy by then.

I went down and down into the eldritch shaft, and in about five minutes the close atmosphere of the place made a decided change. The stale air became dank and humid and I began to notice traces of a cloudy whitish pattern on the rock walls and steps — a deposit of some kind of mold or nitre, indicating that groundwater had found its way into the tomb.

The foetor-spreading steps came to a stop and I was standing in the entry of a large chamber. It was about fifty feet long, thirty wide, and fifteen high. Abominable is the best word for it.

It was partially flooded with black scummy water from the constant seepage of its fungi-clad rocky sides, and not a ray of sunlight or a breath of fresh air had entered it since it was closed in the Eighteenth Dynasty.

I flashed the light at the ceiling and saw a black four-foot square opening directly over the center of the chamber. It was probably the outlet of a pitfall way to hell and gone in the upper recesses of the tomb. More fun and games for the unwary thieves.

I spotted the mouth of another tunnel on the far side of the chamber. And that meant I was going to have to get wet. Very wet. God knows I didn't want to do it, but I didn't have a very appetizing choice. Either I waded the ghastly pool, or I ran that mummy gantlet again.

I started wading.

The inky water was lukewarm and as opaque as split-pea soup. The bottom was a soft mush and I wondered if the pitfall overhead had ever caught any careless thieves and I got all stomachy just thinking about what kind of squelchy old slime I was stepping into. Whatever it was it kept drifting up in thick ropy clots as I waded in deeper and deeper, floating and clogging around my legs, and it smelled as high as the Matterhorn.

It was knee-deep for twenty feet, but there must have been a recess in the middle because after that the soupy mess started to climb on me—the thighs, the family jewels, over the belt and up to the navel. I balked when it reached my ribcage.

Go on, gutless wonder. Show 'em what a man with co-jones can do.

The trouble was, right then my *cojones* were fresh out of manhood. They felt like two shriveled little corn kernels submerged in a leftover bowl of gravy. At one time I had climbed down through the Well and the Grotto in Cheops' pyramid, and that had been bad news but not nearly so bad as this. Thinking about stepping off into a submerged hole and having that bitching black marl suck me down like quicksand was making me a coward.

But I had to stop stalling. Maybe it was just in my mind, but it seemed to me the flashlight was throwing a dimmer beam than when I first started into the descending tunnel. That would do it. Getting caught in that christ-awful place without a light would send me up the walls like a rabid ape.

I started again.

The brackish water inched up my chest, past my shrink-ing nipples, reached my clavicle. I held the flash over my head and foot-fumbled for ground. It went like that for ten feet. Then the gaggly water began to recede — chest, waist, knees. I let out my breath and went sloshing over to the mouth of the tunnel.

It was another dwarf-sized bore, four by three, and it was half clogged with an old deposit of crushed muck. It looked as unhealthy as rampant smallpox and there was nothing I could do about it except cringe. I was still con-vinced I was going in the right direction.

63

I got on all fours and started to crawl. Not far. The ceiling came down and pressed on my back and I had to flatten on my gut. The cake covering the mud broke under my body like the crust on a rhubarb pie and then I was worming into the stinking slime and it was soaking through my clothes and it felt as if it were going right into my running pores.

I snaked on for a few feet, and the ceiling lowered again, and as far as I could see in the feeble light I had only eighteen inches' clearance. The passage curved gradually to the right and I followed it, forcing my head and shoulders around a tight bend, my body squeezing the soft mud aside, which built up on either wall and narrowed the width.

I scrabbled up twelve feet of this viscous keyhole and found I could no longer bring my crooked elbows alongside my chest for leverage. That goddam little tunnel was now touching me on all sides.

Somehow I inched forward another three feet, feeling like the biblical camel that couldn't squeeze through the Needle's Eye, and then what strength I had left turned to rubber and I stopped again.

Everything was wrong. The air — call it that — was like glue, sweat was pooling in my eyes, the ceiling was leaning on my back, and I had my left cheek in that cold oatmeal-like mud.

And then the flashlight began to flicker and flutter and dim.

That's when claustrophobia gave me a nudge. I stared at the hesitant light and I prayed *No please Christ not that on top of everything else.*

Like most field archaeologists, I'm a pretty fair spelunker. But this situation was touching my breaking point. The light was failing, I couldn't keep my face out of that stinking ooze, couldn't breathe, my chest was caught in that goddam vicelike squeeze and the millions of tons of limestone blocks and bedrock and earth were crushing me.

I went a little wild. I tried to shove up, to raise the entire tomb and hill it was burrowed in on my back. I felt like a damp seed buried deep in the warm blind earth. I had to get out!

I suppose the true claustrophobiac can only go insane or kill himself trying to get out of a confined space, but I wasn't geared for either extreme, and the realization that I

64

wasn't Hercules and couldn't raise the tomb even 1/5000 of an inch was what made me rational again.

I laid very still in the slime and forced myself to think about W. H. Flinders Petrie.

Petrie was one of those hardheaded, tenacious Egyptologists who would swim the River Styx and crawl naked through hell's halls to solve one small archaeological riddle. In 1889 he skinned into Amenemhet's flooded brick tomb and unraveled the puzzle of the maze-passages on his gut, with his mouth and nose so clogged with mud that he was breathing only on an Egyptian installment plan.

All right, goddam. If Petrie could do it, so could little David.

I made another wild promise to Jesus and I squirmed, wormed, inched through the ghastly mud, and kept on snaking up and up until I left the last of the muck behind me. Then I could crawl again.

The ascending passage continued for a good two hundred feet before it made an abrupt duck into a long horizontal bore. I went hunching along it like a grinning ghoul hulking out of a graveyard to have a night on the town.

The flash was casting less than a candlepower glow by then, but it didn't matter. I could see a square opening ahead of me and a flutter of light on a far wall. I doused the flashlight and got on all fours again and crawled to the end of the bore.

It looked into the grand gallery. I was just under the corbeled ceiling and almost directly above the hole we had come through by ladder. The stone floor of the gallery was about sixteen feet below me.

Two Colemans were blazing festively at the far end of the gallery and a couple of *fellahs* were industriously banging away at the limestone blocks which had the doorway barricaded. Brandt, Doc, Jeff, Hassan and Anne were standing just behind the workmen in a tense little cluster.

"Hey!" I called. "How about a goddam ladder for the prodigal son?"

ₗ

65

9

I RECEIVED a lot of backslapping and toothy grins, and even Tawwab insisted on shaking my hand. Anne seemed to be in a rapture that I was alive and back in one piece even though I was a mighty grubby piece.

"How on earth did you get out of there? You look frightful!"

"I climbed down to hell and back," I told her. Then I told them about the false rampstone and the forked passages and the mummy corridor and the flooded pit. Brandt was interested in the mummies.

"By God, I'd like to see that. What's a communal sepulcher doing in a royal tomb? Nobody's found anything like that since Christ was a corporal."

"Be my guest." I nodded at the hole I had just climbed out of.

He flashed a grin at me. He had dried blood on his forehead. In the lantern light it gave his ruddy face a barbaric aspect.

"I thought that deadfall got you, fella. You must have been standing right under it. Didn't you notice it was a trap?"

"It looked funny to me," I said, "but I couldn't really tell."

"Perhaps I should take the lead after this," Hassan said. "I'm possibly more at home in these places than the rest of you." He smiled a sort of apologetic smile at me.

Big Brother couldn't have any of that.

"Why hell," he said. "It wouldn't have happened if Dave hadn't been in such an all-fired hurry to get to the loot."

He winked at me so I'd know he wasn't really bawling me out.

"I can smell a trap a block away. You boys just follow Papa after this."

Don chuckled. "You should have seen Farley spring out of that opening when the fall started, Dave. He nearly bowled Hassan over like a nine-pin."

"And a piece of it cut his head," Anne said. "I think he should go have it attended to."

"This nick?" Brandt said. "My God, this is a Boy Scout scratch. Douse it with gin and it's as good as new."

Hail the hearty he-man.

I said, "I need a smoke. Who's got a dry one?"

Anne took me by the arm.

"You come out of here now, Dave. You've had enough for one day. You look just awful."

"But I smell nice, don't I?"

I really didn't feel like joking about it. I felt as if I had been rolled in leprosy and dipped in a latrine. I could hardly stand myself.

"W-ell, you don't exactly smell like a perfume sales-man."

"That's the ticket, fella," Brandt boomed after me. "A couple of slugs of gin and you'll be ready for the ball!"

I took Anne's flashlight and helped her down the ladder into the lower chamber.

"I'm surprised he didn't sing me a chorus of 'Smile, boys, smile.' " I was feeling pretty mean.

"Don't be like that, Dave. He's really awfully nice. And you should have seen him digging at that fall to get you out! He worked harder than ten *fellahs* for two straight hours."

I could see him all right — Farley Brandt stripped to the waist and slinging a sledge and showing all his sweaty muscles. The great grandstander.

She gave me a cigarette when we got outside in the blinding sun, and she took the matches away from me because my hands were going like a pair of free-wheeling yo-yos and lit one for me.

"You're more shaken up than you realize. It must have been terrible for you down there."

"I'll be all right as soon as I've had a shower and a drink. Will you send Yussuf over with one? A whisky. Double."

I went into the shower tent and pulled off my stinking clothes and kicked them into a corner. Then I stood under the perforated tin tub and soaped and rinsed myself for five minutes. Yussuf showed up with my drink and I shot it home in two gulps. It smoothed my jangled nerves the way a housewife can snap out a sheet on a rumpled bed. I told him to take my clothes and bury them somewhere.

Jeff was standing outside in his shorts with a towel slung over his bare shoulder, waiting for the shower. He hadn't said much to me in the tomb, and now he merely gave me that ironic look of his.

"Everything all right, Jeff?"

"Sure. Though I guess we're going to have to be more careful after this, huh?"

"I guess so."

"Funny about that deadfall, wasn't it? How come you couldn't be sure of it? Was it covered up?"

"I don't know, Jeff. I didn't have a chance to see what was above the lintel. I was only half through the opening when Farley came up behind me. So I just squeezed on through."

"Oh yeah? Farley said you told him to watch his step *after* you'd gone through it."

"No. He's forgotten. I said it just before."

He smiled at me. "Well, at any rate it turned out to be a lucky day for both of you."

"That's right. It sure did."

I walked across the parched sand to my tent to get myself a fresh pair of khaki shorts. I felt uneasy. Jeff made me feel that way.

Greta was sitting alone in the marquee with a cigarette and a gin and tonic, wearing a pair of shorts which she had made shorter by rolling them and a skimpy halter made skimpier by folding down the top. She gave me a fixed look.

"Where are the others?"

"Still in the tomb reading the Egyptian comics, I guess. Except for Anne and Jeff. Jeff's in the shower."

"Dear little Anne said she was going to her tent to copy some notes. She's all bubbly with girlish enthusiasm over your great adventure. Sweet little thing."

I went over to the bar and mixed myself a tall highball.

"She can't help it if she's only twenty-one, Greta."

"Did I say anything about her age?"

68

"You don't have to. Your face says it every time you look at her. She tell you what happened?"

"Some of it. Sit down for godsake, Dave. You make me nervous."

"You ain't alone. I'm *real* nervous." I sat down and said, "Well I tried but it backfired. It nearly got me instead of Papa."

"What exactly was it?"

"A trigger deadfall, but not a typical one armed with a load of rubble. This sonofabitch was supporting limestone blocks."

"How did you work it?"

"It was over a small doorway but you couldn't see it from the other side. I went through first, and I even warned him because Hassan was coming up behind him. When Papa started through, I pretended to accidentally bump the trigger post. That's when everything went wrong. I knew I'd be all right because I started to jump clear as soon as I triggered it. But the goddam lintel must have solidified somewhat to the post. It gave a little warning before it let go, and Farley was able to jump back on the other side."

"Do you think he suspects anything?"

"No, I don't think so. I blinded him with my flash just before I did it so he couldn't see what was happening. Right now he's too busy playing fearless leader to stop and think it might not have been an accident."

"What do you mean?"

"I mean he started giving me the Big Brother bit when I got out about how Papa should always lead the troops because Papa knows all about those tricky old Egyptian traps. Papa can smell 'em a mile away with his beagle nose. *Heil!*"

Greta smoked her cigarette. Her pupils looked very small, like little chips of onyx in her dark green irises.

"Well, it's no sin to miss the first time — as long as you didn't get caught. You'll find another opportunity. A better one."

I wet my lips and reached for her pack of filtertips and matches. I knew she was staring at me. I could feel her eyes waiting.

"Well," she said finally, "won't you?"

"Won't I what?"

69

"Dave. You know perfectly well what. You'll find another way for Farley. What's wrong with you? You —"

"Here come the others," I said.

Brandt led the way into the marquee, sweaty and red-faced and boisterous. Doc was mopping at his bald pate with a damp handkerchief. That ovenlike tomb was costing him water weight, but he could afford it. Hassan somehow always managed to look as cool and natty as a bright new swordblade.

"Well, lover," Brandt said, "Dave tell you all about our little excitement?"

He stooped over and gave Greta a noisy smack on the cheek and she stared at me with a set expression. She probably wanted to go wash her face. I wanted to get up and belt him.

"Yes, he did. All about it. You really should be more careful, Farley."

Brandt laughed and swaggered over to the bar.

"Who's for what here? Doc? Hassan? Name it. I'll play barmaid. Well, the truth is, sweetheart, I never did see the bloody thing. But then old Davy was blocking my view, and right at the crucial moment he made a wrong move with his flashlight and I went as blind as a bat!" He glanced over his shoulder.

"Hi, fella. What'll you have? Papa's tending bar."

Jeff walked into the marquee and said, "Gin and tonic, thanks."

He looked at me and sat down across the table from Greta and looked at her. I started feeling edgy again.

"One gin and quin-neen coming up. Smile, smile, smile."

"I'll catch mine later, Farley," Doc said. "I think I'll shower first. I'm as soggy as a Nubian's *djellah.*"

"A workingman's sweat is an honest smell, me lad," Brandt said. He came over to the table with the drinks.

"Tell you, Dave. Me'n' Doc and Hassan put our noggins together and decided those mummies you saw must be the work gang that dug the tomb. It's pretty unusual but that's the only way it makes sense."

"Why is it unusual?" Greta asked. "I thought it was customary for them to seal the workers in the tomb when it was finished, to keep the secret of its location."

"That misconception comes mostly from Hollywood movies, Mrs. Brandt," Hassan said. "Contrary to popular belief it wasn't a common practice; not at all. And here's

70

another odd point. According to what Ferris says, the workmen were not sealed in alive. They must have been dead before they were laid out on the tiers he described to us." He turned to me. "How many bodies would you say are in there?"

"Christ, I don't know. One thing I didn't do was stop to take a headcount. The passage is probably fifty-sixty feet long by ten high, and they're stacked floor to ceiling on both sides. Maybe eighty or a hundred of 'em."

"Strange," he murmured. "A mere one hundred workmen would not be nearly enough to build a tomb of that size. Perhaps we are wrong in our assumption."

"Well, we can determine all that when we crawl down there and take a gander at 'em," Brandt said. "What's the use of worrying? It never was worth while."

"Are you really going down there?" I asked him.

"Hell, yes. A little spelunking like that is good for an archaeologist. Otherwise he grows soft. Hassan and me are going down the way you went as soon as we get the gallery open again."

I raised my glass. "Lotsa luck. I'm not about to go down there again."

Brandt's still eyes watched me over his big smile.

"You don't have to, fella. That's why Papa's here. Hey, where's that Buddha-belly Yussuf? Who's ready to go around again?"

I met Greta in the setback that night, and as soon as we hit the blanket I was half on her and kissing her. I had been too close to death that day and now my still frightened libido had to expand and express its love of living in the most fundamental way it knew. I dug into her blouse and began tugging at her bra until her left breast rolled out, and in the moonlight it looked like a beautiful pale melon and I started to nuzzle it.

"My God, Dave! What's wrong with you?"

"What do you mean what's wrong with me? I thought you liked to be ripped."

"Well, not *every night*. I only brought along so many bras and panties, you know."

"So I'll drive into Aswan and buy you more."

I pulled up her skirt and cupped my hand inside her smooth firm thigh, and then placed it on her soft flat belly

71

over her white nylon panties and the warm silky tactile feel of her went through me like a current.

"Wait, David. I want you to tell me something first."

"Make it a simple yes or no question then, huh?"

"You didn't tell me what you were going to do about Farley."

I pulled up a little, and looked at her.

"I said I'd take care of it, didn't I?"

"You didn't act that way in the marquee this afternoon. You acted as if you had lost your nerve."

"Maybe I did," I muttered. "What I crawled through today wasn't any bed of roses, you know. That stinking fucking mud."

"Don't use that word. I don't like it. Listen, darling. I know what happened today wasn't nice, but it was just a rotten break. It needn't be that way the next time. Not if you're careful, very very careful."

"I don't know that there's going to be a next time, Greta. I don't mind admitting that what happened today kind of spooked me. Maybe what we've been planning just isn't meant to be."

I felt her draw back from me.

"What's that mean? Am I expected to go on living with Farley then? Shall I continue to look forward to having his big sweaty body in bed with me every night? Smelling his gin breath and laying there taking his slobby kisses as he shoves my legs apart and —"

"Stop it."

"—and puts his hand where yours is and mounts up like Julius Caesar on his battle mare —"

"Shut up, goddammit!"

She was silent. We were both silent. After a while she lay back and took my face in her hands and drew it toward her.

"Then what are you going to do?"

"I don't know yet. I'll figure something out as we go along."

"No," she said. "Don't try to play it by ear the next time."

"All right. I'll wait and see and then I'll plan. Something will work out."

"Promise?"

She was looking up at the stars as I lowered my head to her breasts.

72

"Yes dammit, I promise."

I saw her lips tighten suddenly, and then her hands flew up to lock in my hair and I thought she was going to scalp me. She rolled her head from side to side and arched her back and moaned.

"Now," she gasped. "Now tear them off!"

I never did tell her about the other promise I had made that day. The one in the tomb.

10

IT TOOK Tawwab and his crew the better part of a week to break up and cart away the deadfall stones, but they were able to make us a crawlthrough by the afternoon of the third day. We lined up behind the man with the leader complex and wormed into the upper gallery one by one.

"This your false rampstone, fella?"

I told him yes, and reminded him about the north passage in there. He grunted.

"Yeah, but we'll leave that alone till the boys get the gallery cleaned out. Ready, Hassan? Jeff, you coming with us?"

"Uh-uh. From what Dave says, I wouldn't get a chance at a decent picture down there. And I'm not climbing down any tomb's rectum for the sheer fun of it."

"Jeff," Anne said. "Do you have to describe it like that?"

Brandt grinned at her. "How about it, little girl? Want to see the dearly departed?"

I had an idea he would just love to have her go along. The husky hero protecting the frightened little miss from all the ghoulish horrors. She seemed apprehensive.

"Well — I don't know."

"Aw, give it a go. Doc, why don't you come along too? Then if Anne gets spooked, you can bring her back."

"It's all right by me, Farley." Doc smiled. "If you think

73

I'll fit in there. What do you say, Miss Shelby? Shall we show them we're not afraid of the dark?"

"Well —" She glanced at me, indecisively. "Well, all right. I'll try it. But don't be surprised if I start screaming. I don't like close dark places."

They armed themselves with flashlights and Brandt hunched over and led off. Jeff and I watched them go. Then he leaned back against the rampstones and looked at me. I looked somewhere else.

"Think there's enough oxygen in here to smoke?"

"Why not? We can always go outside if the air gets punk. We've got nothing but time. Fearless Farley will probably be down there a couple of hours. We could even go back and have a drink with Greta — if you want to."

Then I looked at him.

"Something eating you, Jeff?"

"Such as?"

"I don't know. That's why I'm asking. You act kind of mute and watchful lately, like a spy in an Alfred Hitchcock thriller."

"Good way to be, don't you think? A closed mouth and an open mind. Only way to learn."

"Learn what?"

"You're telling me, Dave. Aren't you?"

"Am I?"

He chuckled and pulled out his cigarettes and offered me one.

"If we're not careful, you'll be leading with your left again, and neither of us will really know why."

I nodded and lit my cigarette.

"Okay, Jeff. My error. There's nothing wrong with you. Let's take a stroll and see what's at the other end of the gallery."

"Lead on, MacBrandt."

Within fifty feet we came to a great rectangular stepping block of granite. The brute must have weighed in the neighborhood of four tons, and just above it was a small archway which opened into utter darkness. It looked like a copy of the Great Step and keyhole entry to the Antechamber in Cheops' pyramid.

We scrambled over the step and hunched down and duck-waddled through the bore for eight feet. Then we were standing in another dead-end chamber about the size of a large closet. There were no holes in the ceiling of this

74

one. All the walls were solid, plastered smooth and decorated with animal friezes.

There was still a definite feeling of constraint between Jeff and myself, so I took a stab at jollying the atmosphere.

"I know an antique dealer in Cairo who went into Nakht's tomb once. He tells me the friezes you see in there are a real revelation. Most of them depict wild orgies — naked girls dancing on the tables, everybody bombed, princesses throwing up. And he says there's one party girl who has a goblet of wine poured between her breasts and she's holding them cupped up for some soldier to drink out of."

"Sounds like those friezes they uncovered in the bathhouse at Pompeii."

"What it sounds like," I said, "is the only way to go."

"Why sweat it? You seem to be doing all right in the here and now."

I let out my breath and faced him.

"All right, sonofabitch. Are you going to come out and say it or are you just going to keep playing with it?"

"I haven't since I was fourteen. Or do you mean something else?"

"Look, buster. Ever since that night in Cairo when you caught me with Greta, you've been smirking around like a wise old owl."

"Your timing's off, baby," he said. "Don't you mean ever since the day Farley almost caught ten tons of limestone on his bean? You remember — the accident with the deadfall?"

I wet my lips and ran my eyes over him and started to shift my weight. But he grinned at me and held up his open hand.

"Don't Dave. There isn't enough room in here for me to move around. I need a full ring. What I don't need is false teeth."

I don't know. The way he said it and looked at me took the mad out of me. If I hadn't felt so goddam leery about everything I guess I would have laughed.

"Stop bugging me, Jeff," I said. "I've got enough problems."

"Sure. I know. She can do that to a man."

He walked out of there before I could get a chance to ask him what he meant.

I asked Greta about it that night on the blanket.

"Exactly what is Jeff to you?"

"How do you mean?"

"I mean in bed. How else? Twice now he's dropped hints that you put him over the hurdles last year."

"Well, that doesn't necessarily mean bed, does it?"

"It damn sure does in your case. I know you. Now I want to know the story."

She was quite calm about it. She was sitting up with her arms stretched behind her for support, and her bare pendant breasts swayed when she moved. They distracted my concentration.

"Jeff is just a nice boy. But that's all he is, darling. A boy. I was never serious about him. I used him for a while to help me forget that I had to go to bed with Farley every night. That's all."

"That's all? It sounds like a hell of a lot. I assume that you used him in bed?"

She turned her moonglowing head and smiled at me.

"Why are you being so silly, darling? Jeff never meant anything to me. I never loved him. I ended the little affair a month after it started."

"What was wrong? Wouldn't he agree to kill Farley for you?"

She brought her arms in and laid out on the blanket, staring up at the static stars.

"If it somehow helps you to act beastly, then you might as well go ahead and enjoy it."

"I don't get any kick out of the masochist bit, Greta. But I've got to know where we stand. I'm not going through with this business if Jeff already knows that you've been looking for someone to eliminate your husband. And the way he's been acting the last few days, I'm damn sure he suspects something."

"He can't. He doesn't know a thing. Believe me, darling, I've never mentioned the possibility of Farley dying to anyone except you. I never even thought of it until I met you."

I didn't call her a liar because I knew it wouldn't get me anything. I said, "Just the same, he acts funny around me. And I've noticed he keeps watching you too."

"He's jealous, I suppose, poor boy." She put a hand in my hair and ruffled it. "Don't worry about him. He can't

76

hurt us, as long as you're careful . . . Kiss me where I like it."

"Greta. There were others, weren't there? Before me and Jeff."

"Darling, Don't be sulky. Did I ever lead you to believe that I was a vestal virgin? Did I?"

"No."

"Haven't I been perfectly honest with you about my past?"

"Yeah."

"Then why fret about what might have happened years before we met? You certainly haven't lived like a cloistered monk all your life — but I don't worry about it. If you want me, David, then you have to take me the way I am. There isn't any other way."

I took her the way she was.

We started to explore the north tunnel at the end of the week. It was a horizontal passage and the same size as the south bore. Brandt took the lead with a flashlight and Hassan and I followed him, single file, with me just behind Brandt's beefy posterior.

He said oh-oh and stopped dead in his tracks when we had penetrated about forty feet. I nearly rammed my head in his rear.

"The bloody Egyptians are trying to catch Papa with his pants down again. We've got us an honest-to-god pitfall, boys."

He got on his hands and knees and I leaned over his back to get a look. A four-foot square hole was in the floor. Abrupt, sharp and pitchblack the gaping maw yawned hungrily right under Brandt.

I wet my lips. It could happen very easily at that exact moment. A quick stoop, grab both his ankles, snatch them straight up and lever him headfirst into the pit.

Except that Hassan was crouching just behind me with a lantern.

"Who's got something we can drop down there?"

"Here. This will do."

Hassan handed me a piaster and I passed it to Brandt. He held the coin over the center of the pit and let it go. It winked once in the light and was gobbled up in the blackness. We counted seconds, listening. Finally a faint *plunk* came back up to us — an apathetic little sound. The shaft probably dropped straight into the well I had waded earlier in the week.

"I figure about three hundred feet," Brandt said. "Just a nice little stepdown. Smile, smile, smile. Well, we're gonna need some room to move around in in here. Dave, scramble back and tell Tawwab to fetch in some boards for this thing."

I tailed Hassan back to the galley and told Tawwab we needed three eight-foot lengths of two-by-twelve. Hassan was telling the others about the shaft.

"Brandt very nearly walked right off into it," he said.

I glanced at Jeff. He was looking at me.

Doc said, "Farley must have a cold in his trap smeller. That's twice he's almost stepped into something nasty."

"I do wish he'd be more careful," Anne said. "I'm so afraid he's going to get hurt."

"That's right," Jeff said. "You know what they say about the third time being the charm."

I dug out a cigarette. I could feel his eyes on me again.

"I don't think that's very funny, Jeff," Anne said.

"You're right," he said. "It isn't. My mind was on something else."

Once the planks had been laid over the shaft we crawled along the horizontal passage for another forty feet. The bore ducked suddenly and we went down a narrow flight of steps and found ourselves in a large four-pillared hall.

The chamber was unfinished. Portions of the looming walls were roughly hewn; someone had started to plaster them over but had stopped. And some of the paintings of the sun god's journey to the underworld were incomplete. The place gave the impression of work that had been done in great haste, as if the masons and artists had been trying to beat the clock and had lost.

Incongruously, a gold-encrusted bed with legs shaped like lions' feet was standing in the center of the hall. All around it were scattered gold-cased beams and poles which had probably supported a tentlike canopy that had been erected over the bed. And there were two massive gold-covered armchairs, one on its back, the other on its side.

"What the hell is wrong with this bloody tomb?" Brandt growled. "Nothing's ever where it belongs. What's this

78

bedroom furniture doing in here? It belongs near the burial chamber, wherever that is."

"Maybe this is the antechamber to the burial chamber, Farley," Doc suggested. Brandt shook his head.

"Not likely, Doc. There's a wide open doorway over there. Any burial chamber I've ever heard of was sealed up."

"Perhaps the burial chamber is sealed behind one of these walls, Mr. Brandt," Anne said.

"I don't think so, little girl, or we'd probably be able to see some evidence of it. But we'll test the walls just to be sure."

Hassan was squatting in front of one of the overturned chairs, inspecting its arms and legs with a thoughtful expression.

"Look here," he called to us.

The right-angled arms were supported by curved struts made in the shape of three entwined papyrus flowers. Brandt's ruddy face went sour when he saw them.

"Well, boys and girls, that just about queers our chances of finding a pharaoh in here. What do you think, Doc?"

Doc mused over the chair with his mouth pursed.

"Yes," he said, "it's a substantial clue, all right. It indicates that the owner of the tomb was not a king. A pharaoh's chair would show a design of the flower of Upper Egypt as well as the papyrus of Lower Egypt." He straightened up smiling.

"Don't look so downcast, Farley. Where's the old smile? Perhaps we've hit on a queen's tomb. Horemheb's wife might be buried here."

Brandt's beefy face brightened.

"You might have something there, Doc. Hey, maybe she built this tomb the same way she did her pavilion. Just like Cheops' daughter built her pyramid."

We grinned. All of us except Anne knew that salacious old tale about Cheops' daughter. Supposedly she had earned the money for her pyramid by practicing the oldest profession in the world. Her price had been one stone per man. It was a pretty big pyramid too.

Beyond the hall the doorway led to a second hall which had two pillars. Again the walls were only partially plastered and decorated with pictures that had never been completed. At first glance it looked like another blind alley; but the old tomb robbers hadn't been fooled. They

79

had sounded the walls and discovered that the one on the west was false and had cracked open a large hole in it for themselves.

"Those bastards," Brandt said admiringly. "Tell you what. It's going to be a bitch to haul all our gear in and out of that keyhole tunnel over the shaft. So what I think we'll do is put the boys to work in that chamber at the end of the gallery and see if they can't punch a hole right through to the four-pillared hall. That way we can make ourselves a man-sized passage."

He turned and looked at me and I knew what I was paid to do.

"Dave, you trot back and see if you can get some life out of Tawwab, huh?"

I went up the stairs and started crawling back along the keyhole tunnel. When I came to the planked-over shaft I stopped and stared at the boards for a while and gave it some thought. Then I crawled on.

11

"You've found something."

She made it more of a statement than a question, but I wasn't that positive about it.

"Yeah. But it comes with problems."

"Such as?"

"Well, it's a pitfall in a long keyhole passage and right now it's the only way we have to reach the inner tomb. We've boarded the shaft over with planks and it's perfectly safe to use — as long as the planks stay right where they are."

Her teeth flashed in the dark.

"But if the planks were moved —"

I said, "Uh-huh. All I have to do is get on the gallery side of the shaft and push the planks back toward the stairs so that my end will barely be resting on the edge.

Then, when some poor unwary bastard comes crawling along the passage from the hall—zowie!"

"Darling, you're beautiful! I knew you would come up with something good."

"Um. But like I say, there's problems."

"Well, tell me."

"Too many people. Any one of them might take the spill. Doc, Jeff, Anne, Hassan —"

"Then wait. Wait for the right time. Some time when you and Farley are alone in there. It's bound to happen sooner or later. You mustn't chance it when the others are around."

"That's one of the problems, Greta. I can't wait too long. Papa's got the boys pounding out a hole between the gallery and the hall. Once they get that open there won't be any reason for us to use the tunnel over the well."

Greta rolled over on the blanket, onto her stomach. Her bare *derrière* was a pale glowing mound in the crepuscular moonlight. I put my hand on it and worked my fingers in. She let out her breath in an open-mouthed sigh and made her hips squirm, a little, grinding her groin into the blanket and the firm sand under it.

"Don't, Dave. I'm trying to think."

I removed my hand and tried to think too. It didn't work so well for me.

"What's the schedule for tomorrow?" she asked.

"Well, the boys will be working in the gallery. That's all right. Jeff will either be wandering around in the tomb taking pictures or stick in camp and develop what he's already got. There's a good chance of the latter. Anne, I'm sure, will stay in camp and work on her notes because we're not going any deeper into the tomb tomorrow."

"Why not?"

"Because Papa and I have to dope the bed and chairs we found with preservative. That was one of the stipulations of the concession: Farley is responsible for the preservation of all artifacts found in the tomb."

"All right. What about Doc and Hassan?"

"Hassan, you can bet your little thing, will be standing over us making sure we do everything according to regulation. That's his job. I don't know about Doc. He'll probably wander around reading glyphs."

"It sounds better all the time. You don't have to worry about the boys or sweet little Anne, and probably not

81

about Jeff either. All you have to do is wait for the right moment. A time when Doc is either out of the tomb or in some other part of it. Then you give Farley some excuse to go outside, and you move the planks over the well, and you call to him to —"

"Wait a minute, dammit. You're forgetting about the watchdog."

"No, I'm not. I'll take care of Hassan. I'll see to it that he isn't in your hair."

"How do you mean *you'll* take care of him?"

"Just that. I'll get him aside right after breakfast and make up a story for him to drive me into Aswan. Yussuf doesn't know how to drive, and I'll pretend I don't either. Don't worry, I'll work it out. I can manage his type."

I looked at her. I said, "Yeah, but that *is* what's worrying me. How will you get him to do it?"

"Oh for godsake, Dave. What is it you think I'll do? Pull up my skirt in front of him in the middle of camp and say 'Want some, honey?' Stop acting like a silly high school boy. I've been handling men since I was thirteen."

"Yeah. And when you say handle —"

"Oh, shut up. Honestly, darling, you're getting more impossible all the time. We'll never get this thing off the ground if you're going to act surly every time I glance at another man."

I stared at the blanket and nodded.

"Yeah, you're right. I'm sorry."

She reached out and ruffled my hair.

"I'll give you something nice to think about, darling. I mean besides me. The last entry in Farley's bank book is in six figures, and he doesn't owe a dime of it."

That was something to think about, all right.

I don't know what it was that Greta did but when Brandt, Doc, Jeff and I entered the tomb right after breakfast Hassan wasn't with us. Neither was Anne, but we all knew she was staying in camp that day to compile her notes or whatever in hell it was she was supposed to do as Brandt's secretary.

Brandt looked around with a quizzical expression.

"Hey. I feel like a motherless child. Where's the United Arab Republic's favorite watchdog?"

"Taking a day off, I guess," Jeff said negligibly. "I heard Greta ask him to take her into Aswan."

"Yeah?" Brandt put his pale gray eyes on Jeff and held them there. And he smiled. "Maybe she thinks she's giving me my big chance, huh?"

"Big chance for what, Farley?" Doc asked.

"To rifle the tomb, Doc. What else? They don't call me the Pirate of Pharaohville for nothing, do they?"

"Now, Farley."

Brandt's eyes made a quick span over to me.

"The wicked very young and the wicked very old. Greta knows how to get to all of 'em, eh? Well, let's enjoy this day of blessing, now that we're temporarily out from under the judicious eye of the law. Smile, boys, that's the style."

I managed a small smile. That was the best I could do. I had butterflies in the stomach.

It was a real nervous day for me. Brandt and I worked side by side in the hall all morning, treating the chairs and the bed with a chemical substance that smelled like collodion, and by the time noon arrived I was about ready to mishandle myself in public if I had to hear one more run-through of Smile, boys.

Jeff disappeared right after lunch and Doc vanished into the second hall when Brandt and I went back to work on the furniture. At a little after one I straightened up and pulled out my cigarettes and looked around.

I could hear Tawwab's boys banging away on the other side of the hall's south wall. I couldn't see or hear Doc. He was probably totally engrossed with his glyphs.

It seemed to be the moment I had been waiting for.

I lit my cigarette and took a drag and made a face about it, dropped it on the floor and crushed it with my foot, and put a hand to my eyes.

"I gotta get out of here," I said. "Get some air. I feel woozy as hell."

Brandt, bare-chested and glittering with sweat in the Coleman light, glanced at me.

"Go ahead, fella. Get back in the gallery where you can pick up a cool draft. You'll get used to breathing this bloody air before we're done in here."

"Hope so," I said.

83

I walked toward the steps, giving myself a slight wobble in case he was watching me. Out of the corner of my eye I spotted the two-gallon canteen Brandt had set by the cleaning table. It seemed like a good gimmick.

I hunched along the passage with a flashlight, crossed the planks and hobbled myself around like a witch doctor doing a rain dance until I was facing the way I had come. Then I set the flash down and got on my hands and knees and raised the end of the middle board and gave it a cautious forward shove. It slid along nicely, making a small rasping noise. When I had moved it about two feet I ducked my head under and saw that when the plank was lowered it would be resting on only half an inch of the shaft's lip. I set it in place and aligned the other two even with it.

Brandt wouldn't notice they had been moved because the well was still completely covered — and he would have four feet of solid board and stone floor under him before he hit the thin ice. His weight and impetus should plunge the planks like an unbalanced seesaw.

I wet my lips and rubbed my palms on my hips. They were sticky with sweat and grime. Shaky too.

I could kill a man this way because I could con myself into a sophistic frame of mind by saying I wasn't murdering him with my bare hands. No knife, no gun, no blow on the head or deathgrip on the throat. I would simply squat there and watch him walk into a blind pit and I wouldn't warn him. Just a sin of omission.

That's what I told myself and I knew I would have to go on telling it to myself for the rest of my life, and I knew I wouldn't ever really believe it. But I couldn't help it. Needing Greta had made it impossible for me to back out. It was one of those irrational things that happen to certain men when they meet a particular woman.

I pulled back twenty feet from the planks and crouched down. The boys had stopped beating on the wall next door and it was time to call Brandt.

"Hey, Farley!"

"Yeah?" His voice had an echoing timbre in the tunnel.

"Will you fetch me the canteen? I forgot it."

"Right!"

He would probably be groused about it but I didn't think he would question it. More than likely he would assume I had some instinctive prejudice about drinking from the *fellahs'* waterbag which was out in the gallery.

I snicked off my light and watched the small rectangular hole at the far end of the tunnel. The lantern in the hall gave it a soft luminous glow. I stared at it fixedly, waiting for Brandt's massive silhouette to fill it up.

I waited and watched. Sweat began to highball down my face and body and my sight blurred. I scrubbed at my eyes savagely and looked at the end of the passage again. Nothing moved.

What in hell was he doing? Why didn't the sonofabitch come get it over with? The butterflies were going haywire in my stomach and I was so keyed up I felt like being sick right there in the tunnel.

Then I thought, Maybe he suspects. Maybe the bastard followed me up the steps on the sly and saw me fiddling with the planks.

Thinking about it got me so spooky I could hardly stand it. I started to shake like a spastic and I wanted to get up and get out of there. Run — anywhere.

"Looking for me, fella?"

His voice went off like a bomb — behind me. I jumped so fast I clobbered my head on the ceiling, and when I hunkered down and turned around I saw him crouching in the mouth of the passage. He was at the wrong end.

I couldn't say anything. I gawked at him. He was holding a flashlight in a negligent way so that the beam of light struck him under the chin. It made him look like a grinning orange jack-o-lantern.

"Fooled you, huh? The boys punched their hole through the wall just before you called me. So I came out that way to hand you a laugh. C'mon. See what they've done. It opens into the hall just like I figured it would. We won't have to use this bloody tunnel anymore."

I said yeah in a voice that sounded as if it didn't belong to me, and I crawled out of there. I forgot about those tipsy planks.

12

THAT last try pretty well soured me on the whole thing. I had a sort of haunted feeling that something was working against me — some secret force which I couldn't recognize or understand. And I said as much to Greta.

"That's utterly absurd," she snapped. "You're talking like a damn fool. Like a superstitious Nubian. I don't believe in that sort of nonsense, and you don't either. We've just had bad luck. It's as simple as that."

"We've had bad luck? *I'm* the one who keeps sticking his neck out to rig those goddam accidents for him — the ones he merely walks around and steps over as blithely as Christ walking on water."

"Well, I'm still Mrs. Farley Brandt, aren't I? Are you going to call that *good* luck? As long as I'm his wife instead of his widow I'm as bad off as you. Worse, in fact."

"Well, I've tried to make a widow out of you, haven't I? I've done every damn thing I can think of short of hitting him on the head with a pickax."

"Calm down, darling. You'll figure out something and —"

"Kay-*rice*, Greta! My goddam nerves will only stand so much of this crap. Sneaking out here with you every night, worrying somebody will tumble to us, working like a Greek slave in that damn tomb every day, trying to figure out accidents for Papa and sweating over them like I was giving birth, and then seeing them all go blooey in my face!"

"Dave. Will you please stop acting like a frustrated four-year-old? We'll never get anywhere if you're going to fly off in tangents and foam at the mouth."

"We're not getting anywhere, anyhow. I've had it. It just wasn't meant to be."

She drew back from me on the blanket and looked at me with an impassive expression.

"Well — then I suppose that finishes it. At least it was nice while we had it. And we can always think back on it in our old age."

I looked at her. "What do you mean?"

"You know what I mean. It's over. You just said so."

"I said trying to kill Farley was over. I didn't say anything about you and me being —"

"Yes, that too. The one hinges on the other. I'm sorry, but that seems to be the way you want it."

"Now look, Greta. You know damn well that isn't the way I want it."

"But that's the way it's going to be. I've told you I can't go on like this. There isn't any sense to it. It doesn't get us anywhere. If you're going to quit, then so am I. Completely."

"Now wait a minute, hon." I started to reach for her but she pulled away.

"Don't, Dave. I mean it. I'm through."

She stood up, looking down at me. Her hair was like a silver helmet in the moonlight and I wanted to get up and take it in my hands. But I couldn't seem to move.

"And don't stay here, Dave. I couldn't stand seeing you, being around you every day and not having you. Tell Farley you're quitting. Or don't tell him, and just pack up and leave. I mean it, Dave. Don't stay here or I'll —"

She walked off. I sat there on the blanket like an old Indian brave who had been superannuated by his tribe, and watched her go. She passed through the black karoo bushes and became a part of the night. Gone.

And then a funny thing happened to me. I felt like crying.

I didn't quit. I was going to at first — the first thing in the morning. I was going to pick a fight with Brandt and see if I could beat him. But it didn't really matter to me whether I could or not. All I wanted was to get my hands on him a couple of times. Then I was going to walk out.

But I didn't because I couldn't. Greta was in my blood like fire and I didn't know how to put her out. I didn't know what to do about it either. It was a standoff, and it was driving me crazy.

I had no idea what it was doing to her because for three days we never said a word to each other. She treated me like a skidrow rummy who had been salvaged from the gutter by a free bowl of Salvation Army soup. She started talking it up a lot with Jeff during our communal meals in the marquee, and that got me so wild I could hardly stand to eat with them.

Every night I would slip out to the setback and spend a couple of hours pacing in circles and praying that she would come to me. She didn't.

And the days were mean too. I had never enjoyed working with Brandt, and now it was even worse because now I had more reason to hate him. There were times in the tomb when he was humming his goddam smiley song that I wanted to hit him so bad I could taste it. I think if there had been a pitfall handy I would have shoved him into it and to hell with the consequences.

We were all getting edgy. The heat and flies and red dust in everything were maddening enough, but the elaborate intricacy of puzzle passages in the tomb would have had even Flinders Petrie talking to himself.

Beyond the false wall in the second hall we found another staircase descending farther into the hill, which became a horizontal passage and which ended in a pit forty feet deep and fifteen feet across. This pit had been designed for two functions: to trap any groundwater that might enter the tomb, and to confound the thieves. Tawwab's boys bridged the gap and we crawled through a hole the tomb robbers had made in the opposite wall.

Then it really got bad.

Descending passages leading to blank walls. Blind alleys meandering for hundreds of feet and then stopping. Trapdoors opening on to other dead ends. And, cleverly rigged and balanced in the ceiling of one tunnel, a twenty-ton block of sandstone that slid sideways and opened up a bore leading to other empty chambers and corridors which invariably became *cul-de-sacs.*

If it hadn't been for the tomb robbers who had blazed the trail, I don't think we ever would have reached home base. Even so our progress was almighty slow, and by the end of the third day — figuring since we had left the main hall — we were all in a fairly testy mood. Brandt was starting to act like a grizzly with a sore paw, and lately he had taken to treating me as if I were only one step above Tawwab on the hired help roster. It didn't much help my love for him.

"Hey, fella, let's for crysake watch those loose overhead stones, huh? You already nearly put a dent in Papa's head, you know."

That's the kind of thing he would say to me in front of the others. Or —

"Why don't you make yourself useful, Dave, and lay out some clothesline along the way we've come so we can get in and out of here without getting lost every bloody day."

Evidently I was being paid to do a lot of different things, and one of them was to pay out clothesline through half a mile of mazed passages — a job which should have been relegated to Tawwab.

I did it, and kept my mouth shut, but I was thinking, Big Brother, you're truly begging for it.

The next day we found a chamber adorned with unfinished reliefs showing a queen or princess being greeted by the deities Hathor, Anubis, Osiris and Horus. Beyond this room the corridor opened into a huge antechamber supported by six pillars carved out of living rock. Groundwater had risen high in this subterranean room and dirt, brickbats and rubble had puddled together in a crusty muck on the floor. From some of the sorry-looking artifacts we rooted out — broken alabaster, mostly — Hassan concluded that we had reached the chamber where the mummy's funerary gifts were kept.

Brandt's chameleon disposition began to glow.

"Well, boys and girls, I think we're mighty close to the bull's-eye now. Mighty close. If Hassan's right, then the burial chamber could damn well be behind any one of these four walls."

Anne looked puzzled.

"But there are no holes in any of the walls, Mr. Brandt. If the tomb robbers had been here, wouldn't they have found the burial chamber and broken into it?"

Our great leader beamed at her.

"What I'm counting on, little girl, is that they got this far and no farther. No more holes in the walls *could* mean they were scared off before they had a chance to break into the sepulcher."

"Or it could mean the necropolis boys resealed the burial chamber after the thieves had looted it," I pointed out.

Brandt's still, glassy eyes flashed at me.

"You get a kick out of throwing cold water on things, fella? Didn't I advise you to think positive thoughts?"

"My error," I said. "I forgot there's no use in worrying because it never is worth while."

For just a second I had the impression that his gray pupils were filled with a dull red gleam. Then his big ruddy face crinkled in a deep smile and I thought I had only imagined it.

"That's right, fella. That's what I always say. Smile, smile, smile."

I smiled at him.

I left the marquee that night as soon as it got dark, but I didn't go to the setback. I posted myself behind the cook tent where I could watch the others inside the big tent. Anne left for bed about nine-thirty when Brandt, Doc, Jeff and Hassan got up a poker game. Greta came out around ten.

She walked across the moony sand with her hands tucked in her skirt pockets and with her head lowered as if she were concentrating very profoundly on every step she took. I stepped in front of her.

"Greta."

She stopped short and looked up as if I had slapped her.

"Go away, Dave. For godsake go away!"

"I lose, Greta."

"You lost the moment we first met — but neither of us knew it then."

"No. I just lost the fight we had three nights ago. I can't go away without you and I can't stay here and not have you. You win."

There was seven feet of sand between us and it stayed that way. She didn't make a move and neither did I. We stood there like two life-sized Ramesses statues and looked at each other in the moonlight. Then she said, "Are you certain this time?"

"Yes."

"You said that before."

"But this time it goes."

"How?"

"I don't know. But I'll do it somehow. I have to."

"When?"

"Tomorrow."

90

"Tomorrow is Sunday."

"That's what I mean."

"Dave —"

I could have had her then — right then when I needed her more than I had ever needed her. And right there in the sand behind the cook tent, or in the sand before it, or in the sand anywhere. But I didn't. I turned and walked away. Because I wanted her to believe in me, to know I really meant it, to be certain in her mind that I wasn't just trying to talk her onto the blanket again.

It was a bitch of a night.

Sunday was our day of rest. We didn't observe it out of any religious conviction, but only because most of the *fellahs* were Copts — Egyptian Christians of the sect of Monophysites. Doc took them all into town in the pickup. Maybe he was a Copt by nature himself. Monophysite is a comfortable theology for pseudoagnostics inasmuch as it believes that Christ is of the composite nature: partly divine and partly human. The rest of us, I suppose, were agnostics from Missouri. You had to show us.

It was a lazy, stifling day. Anne was napping in her tent, and Jeff was off in a corner somewhere developing pictures. Greta and Hassan were playing double solitaire in the marquee, and Brandt worked on the gin and played kibitzer. I sat in my tent and watched them.

About noon Brandt stood up and gave himself a big stretch and a yawn and walked out of the marquee with his hands in his pockets. He didn't seem to be going anywhere in particular or be in any hurry to get there — just strolling in the sun on a quiet Sunday. He wandered over toward the cooktent, stopped and glanced back at the marquee, then took off through the acacias.

I stayed where I was until I heard his feet slough by in the sand behind my tent, and then I got up and took a peek out the back and spotted him making a wide detour around the camp. Once he was in the open again he laid a beeline for the tomb.

I had figured he would pull something like that — take a jaunt to the tomb when Hassan's back was turned. You can't keep a thieving old dog away from a shiny new bone. I gave him a couple of minutes and then went after him.

All along the descending passage and the gallery and across the two halls I kept ribbing myself up for it, telling myself I could do it because I hated him and that I had to do it because it was the only solution for me and Greta. How it was to be done I didn't know. I would simply have to wing it by the seat of my pants.

The clothesline I had spun along the stone flooring began in the first passage beyond the second hall. I followed it with a flashlight, going down stairs, along a rock-walled corridor and across the bridge over the forty-foot deep drain pit. The white line snaked on and on in the wan light like an endless string of limp spaghetti, making sudden turns, abrupt dips, loping down more and more stairs. It pooled itself finally in a careless coil in a long gallery with a high corbeled roof. That was as far as I had laid the line. Beyond that was the big six-pillared ante-chamber.

I heard a little ringing noise like an *afrit* — a tomb spirit — might be expected to make: *dok dok*. Metal against stone. I switched off my flash and slipped over to the doorway and looked inside.

A Coleman was blazing like a 200-watt bulb, and Brandt was kneeling beside it in the muck and tapping at a white plastered wall with a little sounding hammer. He had his head cocked like a dog listening to an elusive human voice.

I rubbed my gummy palms on my hips and glanced around. Just inside the doorway was a clutter of tools we had left when we knocked off the day before. One of them was a blocky-headed maul.

Brandt was still going *dok dok* on the wall, with his back to me. I hunkered down and reached and very gently picked up the heavy hammer.

I knew what I was going to do. After I tapped his skull I would drag him back to a little chamber where the ceiling stones were loose and ready to give. The *fellahs* had shored it up somewhat with two by fours the day before. I would place his body in there and kick out one of the supports and what those dropping stones would do to his head would obliterate any trace of the hammer blow.

So. It was going to be an accident after all.

I took a deep breath and started toward him, toeing in like a creeping Indian. I stared at the back of his head, mesmerizing myself as I came closer and closer, and his head seemed to expand like a swelling balloon.

Something went *squelch* in the muck under my foot. I froze.

Brandt raised his head. Then he straightened and stood up and turned around and looked at me. His pale eyes were very still and watchful. He wasn't smiling.

13

"SMILE," he hummed absently. "Smile, smile, smile." But he was not smiling. He made a short bob with his head, indicating the maul I was holding in my fist.

"Think you've got the guts to use that, fella — now that I'm facing you?"

The way I stood there all I needed was a dunce cap on my head to make me look complete.

"What?" My voice sounded like one, too.

Then he smiled, but not with his eyes.

"You made a mistake in underestimating Papa, Davy boy. Did you really believe I thought that business with the deadfall was an accident? Hell, it had Greta's name all over it."

"Greta?"

"Uh-huh. How far you think a man like me would trust a wife like her? Just as far as I can see her, fella. I've known for years that she hates my guts and wants to get rid of me. But it's been a kind of fun game to see just how far she would go. I knew she was up to something when she started taking those little jaunts down to the Cairo black market. And when she finally heard about you and went to Giza to get you out of poky, then it was all as plain as the egg on your face."

"How'd you know about that?"

"How do you think? I put a tail on her in Cairo. Good man. Set me back five bills before I could corrupt him into playing I Spy for me. He worked for the government's Antiquities Service and pretended to be from the Survey Department. Catch me?"

"Cobb?"

"Graham Cobb, the boy himself. Didn't you know? I thought you took care of him in Luxor — that phony coronary business."

"No, I didn't know. I had a half-assed idea you had fixed him."

Brandt chuckled. "If that's your story, stick to it, fella. Doesn't mean a damn to me. I don't need him anymore, now that the cards are on the table. And they are, aren't they? All face up. The black queen and the two-faced jack."

"If you suspected so damn much about me, why did you agree to take me on in Cairo?"

"For the sheer hell of it, sonny. I enjoy a tight game. Exhilarating, you know? And I was curious to see what new tricks little Greta had up her sleeve this time."

"This time? You saying she's tried it before?"

His opaque eyes widened in mock surprise.

"You didn't know? She didn't tell you? Ha! What a girl! The foolish very young and the foolish very old. She can handle 'em. All except me. Sure, she's tried it before. But Papa was always on to it. Know what Papa would do? Pitch a big scare into the lover boys and then buy 'em off. They'd just up and disappear, and poor little Greta would never quite know why. Some kick, eh?"

"Some kick."

"You sound bitter, fella. Well, they all do in the end — when they find out where they stand. But you're not quite sure just yet where you stand, are you? Right now you're wondering if she really loves you or if she's just been using you, eh? Well, maybe Papa can help set your mind at ease — give you plenty of time to figure it out for yourself. I'm going to divorce her, see? The fun's gone flat, just like you and Greta. I'm going to charge infidelity. Oh yeah, I know all about you and her in the sand dunes at night. Did you really think you could cuckold Papa?"

I said nothing. He winked at me.

"Papa's getting himself something young and tender. I'm going to marry tasty little Anne."

That's nice. "She could damn near be your granddaughter."

He grinned. "Why knock it? You're getting what you

94

want — half of it, anyhow. I'm handing you my leavings. -She's slightly soiled and she'll be dead broke, so you should make a fine pair of deuces. Speaking of soiled — know where Greta was when I found her?"

"In Paris."

"Uh-huh. Interesting city. Know what she was doing?"

"Modeling."

"Is that what she called it? My, my. Well, I suppose half a truth is better than none. You *could* call it modeling, in a way. You ever pay to see one of those shows they put on in certain quarters of Paris? You and the other customers sit in a little dark room that has a big one-way mirror which looks into a lighted room furnished with just a bed. In a little while a girl and a man come into the other room and take off their —"

"Shut up, Brandt! Shut your fucking mouth or I'll put this hammer through it."

He watched me steadily with those dry eyes of his shining more like polished stones than living tissue.

"That brings us around to my original question. You got the guts to use that thing when my back isn't turned to you?"

I looked at him, hating him.

"C'mon, fella. All you have to do is walk ten feet and raise that hammer. Look. I'll make it easy for you. I'll put my hands behind my back. Keep 'em there, too. How about it, killer?"

I stood there and stared at him and it was like looking into a mirror. We were both seeing the same thing — a thirty-year-old gutless wonder who could kill another man only if he did it from a distance. A cheap tomb robber who had stepped out of his element. And now I saw exactly how far out I had stepped and the sudden realization appalled me. It left me with only one thing to do.

I dropped the maul and turned around and walked away.

"Hey, fella!" Brandt called after me. "You didn't give me a chance to buy you off. Papa always likes to pay for his fun!"

I walked nearly the full length of the inner gallery before I remembered to snap on my flashlight. Brandt's mocking laughter followed me. It sounded very hollow in my ears and I had an idea I would go on hearing it for the rest of my life.

My brain must have been going around like a whirligig beetle, because all of a sudden I woke up and realized I was standing in a dead-end corridor.

"Jesus Christ," I muttered, and I retraced my steps to see where I had gone wrong. I walked into a rock-walled chamber I didn't recognize. Just dandy. Brandt had brought me to such a boil that I had forgotten to follow the clothesline. Now I didn't know where in hell I was.

I took another corridor and started walking and the farther I went the more I thought what would it matter where the stupid thing took me because I didn't know where I was going or what I was going to do anyhow. It was all a grand washout and I knew it. I was through, finished, and the only thing that still amazed me was that I had actually thought at one time I could kill Brandt. Now I knew better.

I thought I knew better about a lot of things. The only trouble was I didn't know about enough of them.

They say God takes special care of drunks and crazy people, and it must be so because in a few minutes I found myself back at the wide drainwater pit. What puzzled me was I couldn't see that white clothesline anywhere. That didn't make sense — unless that prize joker Brandt had reeled the damn thing back into the antechamber for a final laugh. But it didn't matter. I knew where I was now.

Hassan was just starting down the stairs when I walked out of the tomb and into the diamond-bright sunlight. He paused when he saw me coming up and his dark eyes flashed like two crumbs of agate.

"Is Brandt down there?"

It was the first time I had heard him use a sharp tone — and he had picked the wrong time and man for it. I had had my ration of cowcake for the day.

"You've got eyes and ears, buster. Go use 'em."

His aquiline face hardened and his voice was as crisp as frost in a cold snap.

"Don't make the mistake of being flippant with me, Ferris. I have the authority to place you under arrest and I'm quite prepared to use it if I have to. I ask you again. Is Brandt in that tomb?"

Right about then I would have just as soon socked a Department inspector as anyone else. I balled my fists and started up the steps. Then I saw Tawwab chuffing across

96

the sand toward us. He looked all big-eyed with wonderment.

"Please, *effendis*. We are digging today?"

"No," Hassan snapped without turning his head. He seemed about as intimidated by me as he would have been by a belligerent Girl Scout.

"Stop acting like a fool, Ferris. You know my position. I'm responsible for every artifact uncovered in this tomb. And Brandt knows damn well he's never supposed to enter the tomb unless someone from the Department is present. And that includes every member of his staff. It was stipulated in the concession."

"Big deal. So why don't you get your *ghaffirs* and march in and arrest him?"

"I may decide to arrest both of you. Now turn around and let's go."

"Where?"

"Back where you just came from. We'll see what Brandt's up to."

"I know what he's up to. He's tapping the walls trying to locate the burial chamber. Go in and watch him if you want to. I'm going to get a drink."

He didn't move out of my way. His face was almost impassive with set determination.

"Don't make me resort to force, Ferris. I don't enjoy that line of action. I'm authorized to carry a firearm. What must I do to get you to comply — go fetch my revolver and point it at you like a TV gunslinger?"

"Why don't you frisk me?" I said. "Maybe I've got a four-foot statue of Tanit tucked in my shorts."

He looked down at me as if I were an unruly child who wouldn't eat his pabulum, and he opened his mouth to say something.

That was when we heard the scream.

It was sudden and far off and muted. It seemed to hit an abrupt high note and hang there for a moment like something limp, and then it plunged down, down as if dragging an echo in its wake.

"Gee-*sus!*" I hissed. "The planks!"

I had said I wouldn't crawl down the south bore to the mummy corridor and the well again, but I was wrong. I did it because I had to know what had happened to him,

97

and I had to know right then. So I went down into that godawful place once again, with Hassan and Tawwab somewhere behind me.

At first all I saw in the well were those three two-by-twelve boards floating on the black water. Then I saw the tip of a soggy shirttail near the surface. When I waded out and caught it and drew it toward me it became the back of a wringing-wet white shirt, and it dragged along a big balky bobbling weight.

That was Brandt. Face down in the water and very dead.

And there wasn't a thing I could do about my pocket-knife sticking out of his back. Because by then Hassan was wading in the water behind me with his flashlight and he had already seen it.

They were all having afternoon cocktails when I entered the marquee. I remember Anne was standing behind the bar with a martini shaker in her hands, and when she looked at me, at my blank face, some instinctive feminine intuition must have automatically thrown itself in gear. She set the shaker down with a bump and her lower lip sagged. She said, "Farley . . ."

I felt like a little numb mouse. I didn't know what to say. I looked at her, at Doc and Jeff, and at Greta, and said the first thing that came to my mind.

"I'm sorry. Farley's dead. He —"

Greta stood straight up. Her face was like an alabaster funerary mask.

"My God, Dave! You didn't . . ."

14

THE POLICEMAN who drove out from Aswan in a clattery Chevy was a dumpy little butterball of a man. He wore a wrinkled seersucker suit and a cocky red *tarboosh*. His name was Hamel Kebir, and his small obsidian eyes were as enigmatical as a mink's. The first thing he did when he waddled into the marquee was to offer Greta his deepest sympathy.

"My soul sheds tears for this tragic loss of your father, Miss Brandt. A fine man, a great archaeologist. Egypt stands in his debt."

Greta looked at him as if he were a trifle crazy.

"Farley Brandt was my husband. We didn't have any children."

Hamel clasped his pudgy hands in dismay.

"I am covered with error. Forgive my clumsy assumption. But perhaps the mistake is understandable, eh? Such a young and beautiful woman . . ."

Hassan and Jeff took him over to the tomb to see the body. I didn't want to see it again, ever. Hassan, Tawwab and I had had one good-god of a time getting it out of the well. I had Yussuf mix me another drink and I sat down at the table with it across from Doc and Greta. Anne had gone to her tent to shed her soul of tears.

"Kind of a clown, isn't he?" I said.

Greta glanced at me and then looked away and shrugged. She had no interest in Hamel Kebir. I had to give her credit — she wasn't making any pretense of remorse over the loss of her husband. She was as cold as mackerel in a fish market.

I wished to God that Doc would get up and go away so that I could talk to her, but he didn't. He sat there like Humpty Dumpty and looked wistful. I guess he had really liked Farley Brandt.

Fat little Hamel returned in a while and asked would we mind if he used the marquee as a temporary headquarters? And would we please all wait in our tents until he called us? And would we please accept his profoundest apologies for this inconvenience? So kind of us all to be so understanding and helpful.

He saw us one by one, starting with Greta and ending with me. It was seven in the evening when I was finally called. I walked into the marquee and sat down and said, "*Bism' Allah,*" to him.

"No, please," he said quickly. "I am a Copt by conviction, not a Mohammedan."

His *tarboosh* was resting on the table by his elbow and I glanced at it. He caught my look and made a small baby smile.

99

"It's in the nature of camouflage," he explained. "The Arabs in my district have more confidence in me if they think I am one of them. An innocent deception, eh?"

It was then I began to realize I would be making a very big mistake to underestimate this little man. There was a method behind his clownishness.

"Well, well," he said and he fussed over a clutter of papers he had on the table before him. "A great loss, a very great loss. You were his partner?"

"Brandt's? No. I worked for him as a member of his team."

"I see, I see. And you had been with him for some time?"

"No. Only a couple of weeks."

"Ah yes, of course, of course. And today you and he were working in the tomb alone together?"

"No. He went in there by himself to see if he could locate the burial chamber. I went in to see what he was up to."

He looked at me.

"To see what he was up to," he said. "Ah, yes. And then you helped him look for this chamber?"

"No. We talked for a while, and then I —"

"About what, please?"

"Well — about my quitting. I was thinking of leaving."

"Why?"

"Personal reasons."

"I see. And you told him you were leaving?"

"Well no, not in so many words. But it was implied. And then I left him in there."

"And he was still alive then."

I looked at him. He hadn't quite said it as a question.

"Of course he was still alive then. He was still alive when Hassan and I were standing in the entrance of the tomb."

"Why do you presume that?"

"Why? Well, because we heard him scream when he fell into the well."

"You use the word *fell*. How do you know he wasn't pushed or dropped?"

"Well, I assume —"

"A mistake." He smiled a mild, friendly smile at me. "In my business a *prima facie* assumption can be as fatal as an irrational guess. Well, well. We'll come back to that later."

100

I had the bewildered feeling of a man caught in a Kafkalike interrogation. I hadn't killed Brandt, but the ice under me suddenly felt very thin.

Hamel raised a napkin on the table and showed me my open pocketknife. There was still a trace of blood on the slender four-inch blade.

"This is yours, I believe. And I understand you found it in Mr. Brandt's back."

"Yeah."

"I wonder how it got there?"

I let out my breath.

"Well, in this case can't we *assume* that somebody put it there?"

"Forgive me. I phrase things badly in English. What I meant to say was, I wonder how it got from your possession into his back?"

"I don't know. I haven't seen the damn thing for a couple of days. Probably I was using it for something and set it down somewhere in the tomb and forgot it. I haven't needed it recently so I hadn't really missed it."

"I see. And you assume someone else found it and kept it but didn't tell you about it?"

"Yes — if you'll permit me to assume."

He made a gurgling noise in his throat. I suppose he meant it as a chuckle.

"Now," he said, and he was all business again. "You said you left Mr. Brandt in the tomb by himself. And then what?"

"I got bollixed up in the passages on my way out. Some damn fool had removed the clothesline we were using as a guide."

"Ah yes, yes. The clothesline. That's very strange, isn't it? Who would do such a thing?"

"I don't know. But it seems like a reasonable assumption that someone else was in the tomb with Brandt and me. Someone who rolled up the line and planted the knife in his back while I was knocking around in the maze."

Hamel made a steeple with his stout little fingers and looked at me thoughtfully.

"A reasonable assumption you say? Hm. But I wonder who that someone could be? According to their statements the *fellahs* had just returned from Aswan with the doctor and were in their tents, and Mrs. Brandt, Miss Shelby, Mr. Wren and Dr. Ferber were in the marquee, and Hassan

101

Bey and *rais* Tawwab were walking toward the tomb as you were coming out."

I could feel the ice begin to crack.

But it didn't make sense. Someone else *had* been in the tomb, and had knifed Brandt while I was in the puzzle passages, and had stayed in there while Hassan and I were arguing on the entry stair. Then when we crawled down to the well to fish out Brandt's body, that someone had slipped out of the tomb and gone back to camp.

Hamel's little mink eyes watched me closely.

"Interesting problem, isn't it, Mr. Ferris?"

"Yeah. But I still say somebody else was in that tomb besides me and Brandt. Look. How did Brandt get from the antechamber to the well with that knife in him? And why — if he went on his own volition — would he have gone that way? We haven't used that passage in days."

His bright little eyes twinkled at me.

"I really can't say, Mr. Ferris. Until after we hold a post-mortem. At this point I don't know if it was the knife or the well which killed him. I do so hope it wasn't the well. Rather a grisly thought, isn't it? Falling into something like that and knowing it. And that scream you heard rather indicates —"

I said nothing, didn't look at him. I was thinking about the day when I had rigged those planks to topple under Brandt.

"Well, well," he said lightly. "I'll probably be around here for a few days trying to sort things out, as the English say. Perhaps we'll have another little talk."

I was damn sure we would. I had a sick feeling that the shrewd little clown had only started on me.

15

THERE were only five of us at breakfast. Hamel had returned to Aswan the night before with the body, and

Greta had gone with him and stayed there to make the funeral arrangements.

"I don't know how the rest of you feel about this," Hassan said, "but if you think you would care to continue with the dig, I know the Department would have no objection. Their attitude would be quite the reverse, in fact. They are very eager to have this site explored before the High Dam inundates it. And seeing that all the expenses have already been paid, and that we are relatively sure of being close to the actual burial chamber. . . ." He drifted to a diplomatic pause and looked inquiringly at Doc.

"I don't see why not," Doc said. "There's not much sense in us sitting around here moping over poor Farley. And evidently we're going to be stuck here for days while the inspector plays Philo Vance. So we might as well be doing something useful, hm?"

"Sure," Jeff said. "Let's go ahead with it for poor Farley's sake."

I looked at him to see if he was smiling. He wasn't.

"It's all right by me," I said, and we all looked at Anne.

Her eyes were still red from crying and she sat very still and stared at her clenched hands in her lap.

"I don't know," she said in a little brown wren voice. "It doesn't seem quite right somehow — after what's happened." Then she stood up but still didn't look at any of us.

"I don't know. I don't want to think about it. Excuse me."

She made a small fist and put it to her mouth and walked out of the marquee in a head-down hurry.

"Touching," Jeff said. "Very touching, all that sentiment."

"Now, Jeff," Doc said. "You know she was very fond of Farley."

"Sure. We all were. Crazy about him. Ask Greta, the bereaved widow."

"Take it easy, Jeff," I said.

"Take it easy yourself, lover boy," he snapped at me. He started away from the table. "Suit yourselves. I'll be in the tomb if you want me."

Hassan's eyes narrowed with mild concern as he watched Jeff walk out into the explosive sunlight.

"I really should be with him in there," he murmured.

"We all should," Doc said and stood up. "We started

103

this thing together. Let's finish it that way. Coming, Dave?"

"Uh-huh."

I was wondering when Greta would come back from Aswan, and when I would get a chance to talk to her alone. There was a lot we had to talk about. A hell of a lot.

I pointed out the wall Brandt had been sounding the day before, and it should have been the right one because the early Egyptians had had a thing about placing the doorways to their tombs in north walls. Brandt's little sounding hammer was in the muck where he had dropped it, and I picked it up and started to test tap the plastered wall.

Hassan put the boys to work cleaning up the antechamber and they went at it with shovels, clearing away the muddy floor inch by inch. In a little while one of them uncovered some funerary gifts. Most of them were alabaster vessels and were still intact. All of them were inscribed and Doc laid them out on the cleaning table we had set up in the chamber and washed away the old sediment and began mumbling over them.

"They all bear the name of Hrisut," he told us.

Hassan looked like a man trying to remember the words to a song he had heard as a child.

"Hrisut? Wasn't she Smenkhkare's daughter?"

"I think so," Doc said. "Born of Smenkhkare and Meritaten, which would have made her Tutankhamen's niece. There's very little known of her. She probably died shortly after her father did. Perhaps Horemheb and Ay had something to do with it. Who knows?"

He made a face, looking wistful.

"I'm afraid Farley's dream of finding Akhnaten in here is just about over," he said. Then he gave us all a mildly belligerent look.

"You want to know the truth? I feel pretty bad about it. I had hoped all along that it *would* be Akhnaten — for his sake. We all know about Farley. We've heard the rumors regarding his reputation. A cold-blooded tomb robber. Well, maybe they're true. I don't know. But I'm sure of one thing. Deep down in the secret part of Farley Brandt, he really did want to find Akhnaten. Not for loot or profit,

104

but because he wanted to wash his name clean, to make amends for all the graves they said he had defiled. He wanted to quit this world with his name up there next to Howard Carter's."

Doc shut up and for a long moment none of us had anything to say. We stared at the mucky floor and thought our own thoughts. Mine were pretty bleak and they made me a little sick.

Then Jeff shrugged and said, "Well, a mummy princess is better than a mummy general or a priest."

We went back to work and twenty minutes later one of the boys turned up a goldsheeted box inlaid with green malachite and lapis lazuli dragonflies. Doc gave it a bath and read us the inscription.

"Daughter of the King of Upper and Lower Egypt. Box containing deben-rings."

The rings inside the box were a series of anklets which graduated in size to fit a female's leg from ankle to calf. That pretty well cinched it. We had found a princess, not a pharaoh.

One thing looked good for us, though. Down at the west end of the north wall I tapped on a section of plastered block that rang as hollow as Mother Hubbard's garbage can. The others heard it and gathered around me. I ran the tips of my fingers over the surface, back and forth, up and down.

"It's a sealed door," I told them. "Rig up a lamp over here, huh, Jeff?"

I did most of the work in picking out the sealed stones, and as soon as I had loosened the uppermost layer of stone filling I could see that the original seal was still intact. I got all sweaty with excitement then. Whatever it was that was behind the blocked door, it was a pretty safe bet that the tomb robbers hadn't found it.

We pulled out the top layer of stones and stacked them at the base of the door like a curb and I stepped up on them and took a look through the hole with a flashlight.

I was looking into a chamber that hadn't been viewed by human eyes for over thirty-three hundred years. The shadows of weird animal heads danced on the painted walls as I shifted the light, and the dog-headed god Anubis seemed to rear itself out of the darkness as if startled by my intrusion. Little effigies of servants of the dead to do the princess' bidding in the afterworld stood by the huge white-alabaster sarcophagus. It was the burial chamber.

I stepped down with a grin and passed the flash to Doc. He got as excited as a kid after one hurried look.

"Did you see it, David? The lid is still on the sarcophagus. Farley was right. The tomb robbers never got this far!"

"It's a rotten shame he couldn't be here to enjoy this moment," Hassan said. Then he looked at me. "Can we put the *fellahs* to work at grouting out the rest of the stones, or would you prefer doing it yourself?"

I rather liked the way he placed me in charge. For the first time in my life I felt like an honest excavator about to make a serious contribution to archaeological science.

"No, they can do it. There's nothing important about the door, unless we run into another deadfall inside it. Where's Tawwab?"

He wasn't there and no one seemed to know where he was. It was only then that I realized I hadn't seen him since the day before.

Hamel Kebir showed up in the early afternoon, informed us that Greta was still in Aswan, expressed great interest in our find, and spent a couple of hours wandering around the tomb on his own like a fat little ghost.

Around three o'clock he drifted back to the antechamber and asked Jeff would he mind coming to the marquee for a little talk; nothing serious, merely a few random thoughts he wanted to sort out. That's when I started to feel uneasy.

Jeff came back in a while and told Doc that Hamel wanted to see him next. I gave Jeff a wide-open expectant look but he didn't offer a word; just started diddling with his cameras and lights. I would have asked him what was up if Hassan hadn't been there.

When Doc returned it was Hassan's turn to go to the marquee. I gave Doc the same look I had handed Jeff, and he pretended not to notice it. He beamed at the *fellahs* and rubbed his hands briskly.

"Well, I see we've nearly got the door open."

"What's Hamel up to?" I asked him.

"Nothing, Dave. Just a few routine questions."

I didn't like the way he hurried it off. I said, "Such as?"

106

"Oh, nothing vital. Just asked me again about my movements yesterday, and about anything I might have seen or heard."

"Heard? Like what?"

"You know. Anything someone might have said which might possibly be construed as significant." He didn't really want to talk about it. He rubbed his hands again.

"Well, we're about ready to get in there, aren't we?"

"We'll have to wait for Hassan," I said. I didn't much like his evasiveness, or Jeff's either. I felt edgy as hell.

It was nearly five when Hassan came back. He glanced at us and at the opened doorway, and said, "All right, Ferris. Whenever you're ready."

"For what?"

He looked at me. "To enter the burial chamber."

"Oh. I thought maybe Hamel wanted to see me."

He shook his head. "He didn't say so. I believe he's talking to Miss Shelby now."

That made me feel worse.

There was more muck and rubble on the floor of the burial room and we had to have the boys clear it away before we could set up our block and tackle to raise the heavy lid on the sarcophagus.

The lid was a single slab of rose granite, and it was sealed. Our case looked better all the time. The only thing we had to fear now was the fifty-fifty chance that the sacred oils and unguents employed by the ancient embalmers had hardened through the centuries into a pitchy tar which would have cemented the ceremental winding cloths to the body and carbonized its tissues and bones. If that was the case the mummy would be next to worthless.

By the time the boys had a quarter of the floor cleared it was after six in the evening and twilight would be stealing across Akhel Foum. We called it a day and trudged back to camp.

"Where's Kebir *effendim?*" I asked Yussuf.

"Gone, *effendi.* Some thirty minutes past."

I didn't know what to make of that. The fat little detective had talked to everyone except me. I walked toward the shower tent, thinking about the cat that had played with the mouse.

Anne came to my tent that night. Not inside — she

107

stayed in the opening, poised hesitantly like an apprehensive bird searching for seeds on dangerous ground. I was sitting on my cot sandpapering my throat and nerves by chain smoking.

"Dave, may I talk to you?"

"Why not? Come on in."

She didn't. She said, "I have to know the truth, Dave."

"Lotsa luck."

"Please. Don't be flip with me. I have to know. Did you do it?"

I looked at her. "Did I do what?"

"You know. Farley Brandt."

"Oh for crysake. Why ask me something like that? Why *me?*"

"Well — that Egyptian detective thinks you did. I'm certain he does, because of the way he talked to me today, the kind of questions he asked."

"What questions?"

"Well, you know. About you and — Greta."

I stood up. She wasn't looking at me now. She was busy being girlishly embarrassed.

"Why should he ask about me and Greta?"

"Oh, Dave. Don't try to act so innocent. It's too late for it. Everyone knows. You can't keep that sort of thing a secret."

"What is it everybody knows — about me and Greta?"

"Oh, I think we've all suspected for some time that you and she were — were going off somewhere together late at night. And today that detective implied that Tawwab had been spying on you, and that he had told Yussuf, and I suppose Yussuf must have told Mr. Kebir."

I could see the dark dawn of Doomsday. All a cop needs to go silly over in a murder case is a motive. Any cop, anywhere. And now I was suddenly standing there with one written all over me like egg on my face.

"I didn't do it, Anne. It's a fact I didn't like him. The truth is I guess I hated him, or thought I did, which makes it about the same. But honest to God I didn't kill him."

I stepped over to her. She still wasn't looking at me.

"You believe me?"

"Well I —"

"Anne. Were you in love with Farley?"

"I don't know, Dave. Maybe I thought so for a while. I admired him tremendously. Oh, I know what you're thinking. A schoolgirl crush on a father image. Well, maybe that's all it was. I just don't know."

"Did he ask you to marry him?"

Her eyes widened. "Marry him? Why no. How could he? He was —"

"He was going to. He was going to file for a divorce and ask you to marry him. He told me so the last time I talked to him."

"But I don't understand. Why would he tell *you* a thing like that? Why you?"

"He had his reasons. But it doesn't matter now. But if he didn't tell anyone else, and if it doesn't crop up — then you'd better just forget about it. Don't mention it to anybody. It's the kind of thing our fat little Sherlock would like to get his teeth into."

"But I still don't understand why he would tell —"

"Look. Papa was tired of Greta, see? He wanted something fresh and young, like you. Someone who thought he was Christ on a pogo-stick. So he made Tawwab spy on me and Greta because he needed grounds for divorce. It's as simple as that. And he told me because it was his way of putting me down. He was going to hand me Greta on a soiled platter. No money — just his wife in used condition. Now, let's forget it. It doesn't matter anymore."

We were both silent for a moment. Then she said, "I'm afraid it does matter, Dave. I mean Tawwab does. I got the feeling from Mr. Kebir that he thinks you knew Tawwab had found out about you and Greta. He even hinted to me that perhaps that's why Tawwab has been missing for the past twenty-four hours."

16

GRETA wasn't back from Aswan the next day. But Hamel showed up. He came into the tomb with us and he was very friendly and polite. Too much so. I had a sick feeling that the cat was getting ready to pounce.

Doc, Hassan and Jeff had very little to say for themselves. Neither did Anne. I got the impression they were somewhat disconcerted by my presence — the way a polite mixed crowd reacts when someone who has had a drop too much accidentally pops out with a dirty four-letter word.

Little David was definitely being pushed up that well-known creek. And as usual there wasn't a paddle in sight.

Hamel gave the huge sarcophagus a bemused inspection, and then strolled off to haunt the tomb again. Jeff set up a camera by the cleaning table, and Doc and I bathed the artifacts as they were uncovered by the spaders.

There wasn't too much to work with. Most of it was broken alabaster. The funerary gifts had evidently been dumped into the chamber in a heedless haste. It would have made sense if the tomb robbers had been in there before us because they always left a godawful mess behind them. But this jumble of junk hadn't been caused by thieves.

The spaders found a decayed wooden box containing eight cracked alabaster jars and a slender copper dipper. Doc read the inscriptions on the jars and said it must have been Hrisut's make-up box. Some of the cosmetics were *sti-hab* — perfume; *wadj* — green eye paint; *hatet-tjehnu* — Libyan oil.

It gave me a funny feeling handling those toiletries the little princess had used to adorn herself thirteen hundred years before Christ. It seemed to rush all of history's yesterdays into only Yesterday.

A gold-plated chest was uncovered and I recognized it as the canopic chest. It contained Hrisut's vital organs which had been removed from her body during the embalming process and preserved intact. That gave me a peculiar feeling too. They had been functioning intestines once, just like mine. And now. . . .

It was late afternoon when the last of the debris was shoveled out of the burial chamber and we were down to the bare stone floor. The boys rigged the block and tackle over the sarcophagus, the lid was prised loose and a sling attached to it. The lid was eight feet long, four wide, and five inches thick. God only knows what it must have weighed. I told the boys to go ahead, and they laid into it swearing in Coptic, and the tackle began to squeak and creak under the rising load.

110

I heard Anne emit a soft gasp of repressed excitement as the heavy lid swung upward, and then we all crowded around the sides as one of the *fellahs* raised a Coleman and the brilliant white light dashed inside the big alabaster coffer.

It was empty.

We couldn't believe it. All the signs had pointed to the certainty that we would find Hrisut's mummy, and yet we had drawn a blank. Hassan turned to me with a mildly stunned look of disbelief.

"What could have happened? From all indications there should be a mummy here. A sealed tomb, a sealed burial chamber, *and* a sealed sarcophagus."

"I know it. It beats me. I was sure she would be here."

He still couldn't seem to accept the glaring emptiness of the sarcophagus. He appealed to Doc.

"But it doesn't make sense. It's inconceivable that Tutankhamen would have ordered this enormous tomb built for the remains of his niece unless her body was intended to rest here."

Doc shook his head. "I'm sure I don't know, Hassan. I'm as bewildered as you. Unless, perhaps, it's the old story of Cheops' mummy again. A false tomb built to deceive the thieves."

"I can't go along with that, Doc," I said. "If Tut had wanted to keep the final resting place of his niece a secret, he would have built the false tomb at Thebes where it would be obvious — not way to hell and gone up the river."

"Well, well," fat little Hamel said at my shoulder. "Now we seem to have a double mystery, eh? A very old one and a very new one." He smiled his little baby smile at me.

"Unfortunately, my duty requires me to concern myself only with the latter. I wonder, Mr. Ferris, if we might have our little talk now?"

I nodded. "You're the boss."

None of the others said anything as Hamel and I walked out of the burial chamber. It was just starting to darken when we came out of the tomb.

"Now then, Mr. Ferris. I have been compiling and reviewing some very interesting observations and comments

111

since we had our last little chat. The remarkable thing about them is that they tend to form a rather definite pattern. You see what I mean?"

I settled back in my camp chair with my cigarette and iced gin.

"You're telling it. I'm not in any rush to say anything that might incriminate me, seeing that I don't have a lawyer sitting at my elbow."

His oily face showed concern.

"Oh dear. I've been clumsy with my phrasing again, haven't I? Now I've inadvertently put you on your guard."

"Come off it, *amigo*. You always know just what you're saying — no matter what lingo you say it in."

"*Amigo*." He smiled over it. "That means friend in Spanish, doesn't it?"

"Yeah. And I think I could use one right about now. Let's get down to it, huh? You've been playing cat and mouse with me for two days and it's starting to grow a little stale. I know you're wetting all over yourself because you've heard that Mrs. Brandt and I have been up to some hanky-panky, and so it seems to you that my motive for knifing her husband looks like a detective's delight. But I didn't. I probably can't prove it to you but you can put it on record that I said it just the same. I didn't kill Farley Brandt."

He made his gurgling chuckle noise.

"Wetting all over yourself. That would be an Americanism, eh? It's very descriptive." He shook his head admiringly, sat back and put his puffy little fingertips together, and beamed at me.

"Well, well. Now that you've put your cards on the table, I suppose I must follow suit. Yes. It would appear from what I've heard that you had the prime motive for Mr. Brandt's death. Namely, his wife and his money. Quite a bit of money by the way. Nearly four hundred thousand dollars. And of course I have seen and talked with Mrs. Brandt, and therefore that portion of the motive is quite understandable. *Cherchez la femme*, I believe the French say in such a case."

"All right," I said. "So she looks like sex unharnessed. But just because a man goes after another man's wife doesn't mean that he also murders the poor bastard. If that was an invariable rule, there would only be a handful of original husbands left in the world."

112

Hamel gurgled in his throat again.

"Well, well. Suppose we have a look at the cold hard facts, eh?"

He pawed through his papers, selected one and pursed his lips as he ran his eyes over it.

"Let us see now. David Grant Ferris, born 1936, American citizen. In trouble with a fifteen-year-old girl in 1953, ran away from home. Next heard of in 1956 in regard to smuggling antiquities out of Mexico, case dropped for lack of evidence. Uh — 1959, in Greece, convicted of peddling stolen artifacts on black market, served one year. Yes, yes — then in Mesopotamia, 1963, fired by the Jorgenson Exploration Society on suspicion of tomb robbing, no charges, again lack of evidence. Ah! Here in Egypt one year ago, fired for insubordination, suspicion of robbery, and assault against the team director of the Kuban documenting project. And, just six weeks ago at Giza, permit to excavate revoked on grounds —"

"All right," I said. "So you've established the fact that I'm a tomb robber. Just like twenty percent of your countrymen. So what? What's it got to do with murder?"

He raised his bushy brows at me.

"Absolutely nothing, Mr. Ferris. But — if you'll pardon my hasty choice of English words — it does present a rather unsavory picture of an opportunist who excavates graves for illegal profit rather than for the scholarly benefits of archaeology. Is it so remarkable then that someone like myself would assume you would be willing to — uh, dispose of a man like Mr. Brandt for the sake of nearly half a million dollars?"

I raised my brows back at him.

"Ah-ah. An assumption can be as fatal as an irrational guess."

He gurgled delightedly.

"Touché! I believe that is the French word for it? Well, well, no matter. We have established the pattern of your past. Let us now delve into your present." His small bright eyes shot at me.

"You admit that you have been holding clandestine meetings with Mrs. Brandt? I mean prior to her husband's death?"

"You're still telling it. And I'm still sitting here without legal counsel."

"Come, come, Mr. Ferris. Upon severe questioning,

113

Mrs. Brandt has admitted to me that you and she were having an affair, and that you had discussed with her the possibility of her husband having — shall we say — an accident in the tomb."

I managed to force up a smile for him.

"You've been seeing too many American crime movies on TV. That trick of playing one suspect against another went stale in Al Capone's day."

"Al Capone? Ah! The famous beer baron in your Prohibition era, eh? Yes, I remember. But seriously, Mr. Ferris. I do have the statement of the servant Yussuf here somewhere — and it states that the head *rais*, Tawwab, informed him that you and Mrs. Brandt were in the habit of meeting in the sand dunes at night. True, true, it is only hearsay evidence. But do you deny it?"

"Without legal counsel I don't deny or confirm. But I still say so what? It wouldn't prove I killed her husband."

"But the pattern, Mr. Ferris. The further it unravels the more apparent it becomes. So far as we know, *you* were the last person to see Mr. Brandt alive. You have admitted that *you* were alone with him in the tomb. It was *your* knife we found in his back —"

"But I didn't put it there. And I god sure didn't dump him down that well. Hassan was with me when that happened, remember?"

"Yes, but there's an explanation for that. Our coroner says the knife blow was delivered between the ribs and given a slight twist to let air into the wound. Had the blade been a little longer it would have penetrated the heart. As it was, Mr. Brandt did not die immediately. The assailant probably left him for dead, but in a little while Mr. Brandt, who appears to have been an extremely hearty man, recovered and began to crawl out of the tomb for help. But, in his daze of shock and pain, he must have forgotten to take a flashlight — and, as we already know, someone had removed the guide line. So poor Mr. Brandt, hemorrhaging to death and lost in the dark, unwittingly took the wrong exit from that large pillared hall and crawled onto those planks covering the pitfall."

He leaned back in his chair, watching me.

"Isn't it strange those planks gave under his weight so easily? They are twice the length of the opening of the shaft. It almost leads one to suspect that the planks had been tampered with, eh?"

114

I said nothing. He hunched forward, his eyes intent on me.

"Hassan Bey has stated that when you and he heard the scream in the tomb, you cried, 'Jesus, the planks.' Now what made you automatically assume that Mr. Brandt had fallen through those planks, Mr. Ferris?"

"Well, because that's what it sounded like. Like a man falling from a great height and screaming about it. And that three-hundred-foot shaft was the first thing I thought of."

"Then why didn't you say, 'Jesus, the shaft'? You see my point? I don't understand why you instantly specified those planks. Unless of course you already knew they were unsafe."

I wet my lips. "I don't know why I said it. It was just the first thing that popped in my head."

He stared at me for a moment, then said, "I see. Well, let us get on to another interesting point. According to the statements of the others, when you came to the marquee and informed them of Mr. Brandt's death, Mrs. Brandt jumped to her feet and cried, 'My God, Dave, you didn't.' Now what would make her say that?"

"How in the hell would I know?"

"Why do you *think* she would say it?"

"I don't know."

"No? Really?"

"No. Really."

He pursed his baby mouth and looked pouty.

"Hm! I wonder what she meant by 'you didn't.' You didn't what?"

"Why don't you ask her?"

"I have, Mr. Ferris, but she seems rather evasive about it. Says she doesn't really recall saying such a thing, and claims she has no idea why she *might* have said it. The truth is, she has been rather vague in answering every question I have put to her. Almost as if she were covering up something — or covering for *some*one."

He looked at me expectantly, but I didn't give him any help and he raised his heavy black brows resignedly.

"Well, well. There's still one more point we haven't touched upon. The late Graham Cobb."

"Is he supposed to be part of my pattern too?"

"I'm afraid he is. Yes. Mr. Cobb's body was sent to Cairo last week. When I learned of his untimely death

115

from Doctor Ferber I requested an autopsy, and I received the coroner's report last night. It seems that the death certificate, signed by a certain American proctologist in Luxor, was erroneous. Mr. Cobb did not die of a heart attack. In fact he had no coronary history at all. It was revealed, however, that he had enough apocynin in his system to stop twenty hearts. Do you know what apocynin is, Mr. Ferris?"

"No."

"It comes from a poisonous plant belonging to the dogbane family which grows wild along certain sections of the Nile. In this particular instance a kernel of the fruit of the *Tanghina venenata* was used, which is one of the most deadly of the order. An overdose paralyzes the heart by overstimulation."

He tilted to one side and probed a fat hand in his coatpocket, brought out a dark seed that looked like a brown bean and placed it on the table where I could admire it.

"Innocent looking, isn't it? But if you dissolve it in food or liquid it is sufficient to kill twenty men." His eyes blinked at me.

"I found four of these little kernels here in this camp. Can you imagine where?"

I let out my breath and leaned forward and mashed my cigarette in an empty saucer.

"In my pillow."

"No. Rolled up among your spare socks. I took the liberty of going through your tent today while you were in the tomb. My duty — you understand, of course."

It was time to go. If I'd had any sense I would have gone the night before after I had talked to Anne Shelby. And now it was nearly too late.

"It was planted," I said.

"Yes, I rather felt you would make that reply. The same way you claim that someone else used your knife on poor Mr. Brandt." He gave a heavy sigh and looked a trifle distressed.

"Really, Mr. Ferris, don't you think it's about time you were honest with me? A voluntary confession might stand in your favor later on. Otherwise — our courts can be unpleasantly harsh in matters of homicide."

"Are you arresting me?"

"I am afraid I must. Yes. The evidence leaves me no other course. I am very very sorry, Mr. Ferris."

116

He made a motion to scoop up the little brown bean but misjudged the distance. The kernel bounced from his fingers, rolled rapidly and popped over the edge of the table.

He said, "Oh dear," and leaned down to find it.

I had a pretty good idea how much of a chance I was going to stand in a UAR court with a Copt judge, an Arab jury, and a Turkish lawyer. It was definitely time for me to decamp.

I stood up, leaned over the table and threw a right jab just under Hamel's ear. It was a good blow. It toppled him out of his chair and he hit the ground in the womb-curled position and stayed that way.

If you've murdered one man it doesn't much matter to you if you kill another. But if you've never killed anyone, then it means a hell of a lot if you knock a man down and he doesn't make a move. I took the time to feel his pulse and listen to his breathing. He was doing as nicely as could be expected.

I went behind the bar and got a pint of Old Overholt, and then I got out of there.

Night's vast spangled dome was over Akhel Foum and all the little lantern-lit tents were glowing like a cluster of roosting fireflies. Some of the *fellahs* were playing trick-track in their quarters and the clatter of the backgammon pieces and the monotonous drone of their chatter had a lulling, everyday sound that clashed with my mood.

I went into my tent, found a jacket in the dark, stuffed a couple of chocolate bars in it for energy, got my money and went out the back of the tent and through the black and silver criss-cross of the acacia shadows, and kept on going, first into the karoo bushes, then slogging over the rising drift sand, and then into pebbles and rocks and flints, and finally into a shallow ravine which was a dry watercourse and which would take me into the hills.

I stopped and looked back.

The snug, sparkling little camp looked warm and self-contained, totally independent of the outer world. And suddenly I felt like a castaway stranded on a bare coral hump in a receding sea. It was a sensation I hadn't felt in thirteen years — and right now was the wrong time to have it come back on me.

Run, gutless wonder.

117

I walked into the dark ravine, into the still, overripe shadows. In a little while I started to whistle. But it didn't help. I was scared.

17

I COULD easily have snitched one of the cars or the pickup, but all I would have gained by it would be a short running start. There just aren't enough through roads in Egypt for an oldtime cops-and-robbers highway chase. The law would have had me bottled up in roadblocks as tight as Hrisut's colon in her canopic chest.

I decided to stick with the Nile.

I would hoof it north for a few miles and then cut over to the river at Garf Husein and buy myself an off-the-record ride on a northbound *felucca* or a cargo boat. The natives around Garf Husein were pretty friendly toward me because I used to get on well with some of their daughters and sisters when I was working at Kuban — and Copt peasants can always use a few extra piastres.

If I could just reach Cairo, I was sure Sordo would find a way to get me out of the country. That old thief had more shady connections than you could shake a stick at.

That was how I had it figured when I started up the ravine, but it didn't pan out that way.

I had only gone a couple hundred yards when a sudden clacking in the dry pebbles stopped me. Three gaunt, mangy-looking jackals were slinking around in the rocks just ahead of me. Their down-slanted eyes dripped liquid fire in the starlight as they stared at me fixedly. A long black object like a tree trunk was prone on the ground in front of them.

"*S'git!*" I hissed and pegged a stone.

They swung away, tongues lolling, hindquarters drooping, tails slung under, whining piteously. I went over and looked at the black object lying on the pebbles.

It wasn't a log. But he was as dead as one. The smell said so.

I struck a match and hunkered down for a better look.

The only way I could tell it was Tawwab was from his clothes. The bastardly jackals had eaten away his face. He had been strangled. Someone had put a thin leather belt around his scrawny neck and pulled it through the buckle as tight as it would go.

It was my belt, of course. That was one of the rules in this crazy business.

I got up wind of him and sat down on a boulder and dosed myself with the pint.

I looked at him, lying there in the dirt like something nobody could care less about, and I realized it was time to change my thinking. About everything. Beginning with that fifteen-year-old girl when I was seventeen and stupid and got caught and when I first started to run. Because I hadn't really stopped running since. Not until this moment.

But just sitting there and telling myself I had stopped didn't give me the means to fight back. I didn't know who I was supposed to fight because I didn't know who had built a frame around me and hanged me in a dark corner.

I worked on the pint some more and kept looking at Tawwab.

"I don't know, Tawwab. It just won't make sense."

Effendi?

"At first I thought maybe Brandt had gotten rid of Cobb because he intended to rob the tomb. But now I don't think he was planning that at all. And he had no reason to kill Cobb because Cobb was spying for him just like you were, and anyhow we know he didn't kill himself and he didn't kill you."

No, effendi.

"No."

I had some more rye and started to warm up to my theme, using Tawwab's mutilated corpse as a sounding board.

"So what we need is somebody who had a motive that connected him to Cobb, Brandt and you. Somehow all three of you gave him motivation because you were standing in the way of his goal."

119

Yes, effendi!

"Yeah. Now we don't know what his goal is, but maybe we don't have to know to see a glimmer of daylight. If we can just sort out the pieces maybe we can see the pattern. Fatboy Hamel believes in following a pattern, and archaeologists work the same way. They spade and sift and study and slowly piece together a pattern of the past."

Good, effendi.

"I think so. So what obvious pieces of the potsherd do we have to fit together? We have you and Cobb. You were both spying for Brandt. So obviously you both saw something that someone didn't want you to know about."

True, effendi.

"Yeah. But the only trouble is you were both spying on me and Greta. And if we eliminate me, that leaves Greta. And that doesn't make any sense because Greta was out of the hotel the night Cobb got the poison, and she was in the marquee with the others when Brandt was knifed, and I can't picture her luring you out here and choking you to death with my belt."

No, effendi.

"Christ. The pattern isn't worth a goddam."

Unless, effendi —

"Unless you and Cobb just happened to stumble onto someone other than me laying Greta."

Good, effendi!

"Yeah! And whatever it was you couldn't have seen it together because Cobb was killed in Luxor while you were in Akhel Foum. So each of you had a separate piece of information concerning the killer — and he knew you had it and knew it would queer his plan if he didn't take care of both of you. And that means Cobb knew something that would prevent him from killing Brandt with impunity — and *you* knew something else that would prove he had killed Brandt."

Ah! Effendi!

I scooped out a shallow bed for him in the sandy bottom and covered him up with a mound of big stones to keep the jackals off him. I didn't remove my belt from his neck because I had an idea it no longer mattered. At least I hoped it wouldn't.

I didn't go to the Nile. I stayed in the lonely hills and

laid a wide circular track around Akhel Foum. I did it that
way because I had to stall for time. I was afraid Hamel
might have put the *ghaffirs* on my trail and I wasn't ready
to be caught just yet.

It was a mean night, and God knows I could have used
one of Jeff's amphetamine pills. I couldn't risk curling up
in a bush for a couple of hours of shut-eye because I had
put down a hippopotamus trail that a myopic cub scout
could have followed. I had to keep on the move if I didn't
want to be nabbed.

The farther I went into those meatball hills the more I
felt I was about to go over the edge Columbus' sailors were
afraid of — deep into a wilderness of rocky canyons and
barren hills glowing in the cold starlight like mounds of
scrap iron.

My boots sent echoes up the gorges which died of loneli-
ness away up the towering cliffs against the sky. A kicked
pebble would rattle across the rocks with the disturbance of
a rat in a tomb, and every time I paused to listen the silence flowed around me in a pressure that seemed to hurt
my ears.

A moon that looked moldy started sneaking over the
high-hung sky, shedding wan beams through the break in
the naked peaks, touching the crouching rocks which were
mounded like slag along the pass with a gelid radiance that
looked as cold as witch-shine. A few miles of walking by
myself in that solidified million-ton hush and I was suffer-
ing for companionship as avidly as thirst. There was no
water — only calcined cliffs and emptiness. I might have
been the first man inside those fissured hills since the time
of Exodus. It made me feel insignificant, vulnerable, little-
boy-lostish, as if I could sense some great anachronistic
pterodactyl crouching among the skyscraper walls of stone,
hissing and clacking to itself, watching me hungrily.

I guess I was also a little drunk.

I finished the last drink at two a.m. and pitched the dead
soldier against a rock just to hear the noise. Then — as if it
had been waiting for just that to happen — a denser darkness shifted out of the Red Sea and the canyons were blot-
ted by India ink. There wasn't a star in that blackness or a
moon. A husky wind eddied and moaned through the crags
causing an upper layer of sand to blow overhead, and the
firmament was blanked out. It smelled sulfureous and
smothering.

121

I blundered across the clinker-like floor from boulder to boulder until I realized I was going to get myself so turned around in that funhouse I would never find my way out. I hunkered down in a rocky niche and wished I hadn't been such a pig with the rye and tortured myself thinking about the cigarettes I couldn't have because I was afraid to strike a light. I just sat there and listened to the bitchy wind and felt sorry for myself. It wasn't much fun.

Dawn was up three hours later and I got up with it and tramped down through the fissured foothills toward the Nile. Sunrise was slanting ochred shadows across the flinty earth and shooting silver sparks out of the scrap iron rocks and sending long bright spearheads across the valley floor. The river in the distance was a ragged thread of lime, and not far from the shoreline a saffron fog was banked up under the ripening sky to blot the Eastern Desert.

I figured the law would probably be beating the hills for me and it seemed like a good time to leave them and double back to Akhel Foum. But my timing was off.

The shrinking foothills opened alarmingly onto a great flatland facing the Nile which was a crosspatch of agricultural fields and shallow drainage ditches. And I could hear a car coming down the Akhel Foum road.

I stood there for a moment like Lennie the loony and didn't know what to do. I couldn't go straight ahead, into the open, and I didn't want to go back into the hills and run headlong into some trigger-happy Arab cop. Then I spotted a cabbage field off on my right.

I hotfooted toward the center of the field and threw myself flat on my gut on the baked clay earth and pretended my head was just another cabbage. Seemed to me it should pass for one if seen from a distance.

Hamel's bronchial old Chevy wheezed out of Akhel Foum and came to a steamy halt midway between the pass and the river. There armed *ghaffirs* and two Egyptian policemen got out and stood in a huddle in the road. I could see them pointing indecisively in different directions but couldn't hear their voices. Finally they split up and began to beat the skimpy hedges and scout the drainage ditches. As far as I could see they never once concerned themselves with the cabbage field proper. It must have looked so obviously empty in its open flatness.

I watched them in bits and pieces for over an hour and it was a bad time. The ground wasn't dirt, it was sunbaked

122

clay and it was hard. And the rising Egyptian sun scorched it like a greaseless griddle. And there were cabbage bugs. They wanted to get into my ears and clothes and one of the little bastards did get into my hair and there was nothing I could do but let him enjoy himself because I was afraid to move my arms. And I had to go to the bathroom. Naturally.

The defenders of the UAR came together again on the road, about a hundred yards from my position, and held another confab. From all appearances they decided to give up the search — at least in that locality. They tramped back to the Chevy and took off toward the Nile like Gang Busters.

Not a moment too soon. I stood up and watered one of the cabbage heads and said, "Take that, you buggy thing." Then I turned away from the river and started up the Akhel Foum road.

That morning hike back to the valley showed me what a mistake I would have made if I had tried to hoof those hills in daylight.

Heat! There wasn't a breath of air or a stir of life as far as the eye could see. Creeping fissures had cracked the floor of the pass and the canyon walls sheared up as silent and bare as deserted temples. Ashes. That's what the place made me think of. Dead ashes. Even the air was dead. Heat rained down through a silence as quiet as deafness, and the rocks lay around on shelves of granite and sandstone like parts of a tyrannosaurus fossil. Eastward where the sun was climbing, as if in a hurry to cause more devastation with its bloodstained eye, the inner range of jagged hills hulked up like the roofline of a war-torn town.

I left the road when it started to empty into Akhel Foum and drifted off to one side to skulk through the heaped drift sand. The camp looked wan and abandoned under the blistering sun — lifeless, as if it and the atmosphere both were petrified. It would seem that I had drawn the law out of there. It was nearly eight when I slipped down the steps and into the silent tomb.

I stood still in the entryway and did some intent listening but couldn't hear any sounds of life in there. We kept a toolbox in the mouth of the passage and I helped myself to

123

a flashlight and went up to the grand gallery and drank about a quart out of the *fellahs'* waterbag. Then I went on in to where the puzzle passages began and selected a small chamber to the right of the clothesline, sat on the floor and followed a gooey candy bar with a cigarette. I had some more thinking to do.

The way I saw the pattern now, it fit only one person.

My reasoning was illogical as hell because I still couldn't pin down his motive. But obviously he had known about *my* motive from the very beginning and had made me the scapegoat to cover his murders right down the line, one, two, three.

Cobb, Brandt, Tawwab.

Why had he killed them? What could he gain by it? Brandt had to be his prime target, otherwise he couldn't have used me and my apparent motive as a red herring. So Cobb and Tawwab then must have been unavoidable kills that he hadn't originally planned on — but they had come in handy to help pin the main event on me and to divert suspicion from himself.

All right. Take Cobb and Tawwab.

Graham Cobb had known that Greta had picked me out of a jail. And Graham Cobb had died. But it couldn't have been for that reason because that helped to establish my motive for Brandt's death. And why would the killer want to get rid of a witness who could work in his favor? No. Cobb had known something else about the killer, and that was why he had died.

And the same with Tawwab. He had known I was meeting Greta on the sly at night. And he had died. But not for that reason, because again it would be senseless to kill a man who could have appeared against me on a murder charge.

As far as I could see there was only one explanation, and it hinged on that poor grinny bastard Tawwab. And the killer had known that.

But still — What did he gain by killing Brandt?

That was the big stumbling block. The Why. Without a motive how could I prove he fit the pattern?

I flicked on the flash and looked at my wristwatch. Nine minutes to seven. Yussuf would be toting the breakfast to the marquee about now. Thinking about ham, flapjacks, sunny-faced eggs and coffee—especially coffee—didn't do

124

me much good just then. I gave myself another cigarette and it tasted like an old family Bible page.

I was pretty sure that what was left of Farley Brandt's team wouldn't do any work that day. In fact, other than for some last-minute documentation, they would probably seal up the tomb next week and call it quits. Just like my mice and men type plans, the entire dig was more or less a washout. The Aswan High Dam could have it.

But I had a hunch that at least one person would show up.

Because it fit his pattern.

I was certain I could take him, and it was the only possibility I could think of. I would have to beat the motive out of him.

But I was wrong. It didn't work that way at all.

The muted echo of footsteps funneled along the meandering corridors. I made like a listening bird dog. Two people were following the clothesline. I crawled over to the doorway of the chamber and put my back to the wall and concentrated on their oncoming voices.

One of them belonged to Hassan. The other was Greta's.

18

"AND SO this is what all the fuss has been about."

Greta said that. She and Hassan were standing by the sarcophagus in the burial chamber. I was against the north wall in the antechamber and the light from their Coleman was spilling through the doorway by my feet.

"That's it, I'm afraid," Hassan replied. "An old frustrating story to Egyptologists. No mummy and few artifacts. The sad culmination of archaeological endeavor."

"But from what the others have told me, you were all certain the mummy would be here. Not that I really give too much of a damn, but why isn't it?"

"I've given that a great deal of thought. All the clues are here and it's only a matter of placing them into a logical pattern. To begin with, your husband's research was based on a false assumption. He thought we were digging into Akhnaten's tomb. Later we discovered it belonged to Hrisut. Had we stopped to check back on Hrisut we probably would have found that she had originally been buried in the Valley of the Kings or thereabouts."

"Originally? I'm afraid I don't understand."

"It's really quite simple. Assume that Hrisut died during the reign of her uncle Tutankhamen and was buried at Thebes, which would be proper. Then the thieves broke into her tomb, probably at night and no doubt in a great hurry because they only took the small portable articles of value. And of course they took her body, knowing that the most precious objects would be concealed in her winding cloths. God only knows what they did with the mummy then.

"Now it's my theory that when the official who was in charge of the necropolis reported to Tutankhamen that the tomb had been defiled, he didn't have the courage to tell Tut that his niece's body had been stolen. So the outraged Tut, fearing a second violation against his niece, must have ordered that she be reburied in a secret tomb here at Akhel Foum — not suspecting that Hrisut's sarcophagus was empty.

"Tut must have specified a labyrinth tomb, and he probably came here on an inspection tour. Satisfied that everything was proceeding to his liking, he then retired from the scene. And from that point on the frightened official gave orders for a hurried completion of the job. No doubt he was in a great sweat to get the empty sarcophagus safely out of sight as quickly as possible. And that's why we find so many unfinished walls in here.

"Still working under pressure, our harassed official literally dumped the funerary furnishings into the antechamber. And then he arrived at the big problem. The huge sarcophagus could not be hauled into the tomb in one piece. This meant that the one hundred workmen who had to handle the coffer knew it was empty. That wouldn't do. The secret would soon be out and his desperate game of deception would be known. So, once the sarcophagus was in here and resealed, he had the poor souls poisoned, and placed their bodies where Ferris found them.

126

"Finally, when the rest of the workmen were plugging the entry with rubble, it was discovered that some inscribed potsherds from Hrisut's original tomb had been left out. These they simply tossed in before they sealed the tomb and covered up the stairs. And that is just about it."

"Except that other thieves broke in here later on," Greta said.

"Yes. And that presents a logical pattern too. They knew exactly where to go and what to look for. Evidently they had no problem with the traps and tricky passages. And you notice they only came as far as the antechamber. That suggests one thing: they didn't bother with the burial chamber because they knew the mummy was gone. Actually there wasn't much of value left that was portable. Apparently they carried the bedroom furniture as far as the first hall, and then abandoned it when they realized it would be too much work trying to get it through the keyhole passage. Later this second violation was discovered and the thieves' bore in the entry passage was replugged. And that's how it remained until we came along."

"You really enjoy this sort of thing, don't you? In a way I think you actually live it."

"Yes, I do." His voice took on a quiet euphonic quality. "But not for the reason men like your husband or Ferris dig. I've never been interested in the financial rewards. Too many people even today still persist in believing that the primary object of archaeology is to uncover old artifacts which are valuable to collectors. They can't seem to realize that it isn't the artifact itself which is of value; it's what the artifact can tell us of the past that is important. The true archaeologist is a detective. He searches for facts in order to establish a historic truth. And an accurate history is vital to mankind. Without it man has no conscious past. He is like an ape gibbering in a tree without any conception of what has transpired in the world before his time. It leaves him guideless and without incentive to progress."

"Speaking of incentive . . ."

Greta's voice was as low and throaty as a cat's purr. There was a short static silence. Then her voice again — harsh and hissing.

"Tear me! Tear me!"

It was like being hit over the head in the dark.

I stood there in a kind of mental paralysis, gawking at the shadowy wall across the room, at a larger-than-life painting of a naked girl playing a lute. I remember her skin was a rich carmine.

Then something clicked and the wheels resumed their rotation.

Of course, his motive had to be the same as mine. Otherwise he wouldn't have gained a thing by killing Brandt. Farley Brandt's death bequeathed two endowments: his money and his wife, and they went together like Siamese twins. I hadn't been able to see it because my self-conceit wouldn't let me admit to myself that she didn't love me.

My heart clubbed up and took a wild swing, and I wanted to break loose like the scourge of God and cause fire and rape and unmitigated slaughter all the way to the Mediterranean Sea.

I shoved away from the wall and stepped into the lighted doorway and stopped. They were standing on the far side of the open sarcophagus, wrapped up like a pair of prehensile squids and chewing each other's faces.

"Start with her bra and work down," I said. "That's the way she likes it."

If I had seen them jump the way they did in a movie I probably would have laughed. But having seen them pawing and mouthing each other in reality before they sprang apart didn't strike me as very funny. It was the only time I ever actually saw Greta lose her composure. Her blouse was opened over her outthrust white brassiere and she clawed it together with one hand and clutched at the edge of the alabaster sarcophagus with the other. Her dark green eyes looked very wide and luminescent in her pert pale face, like one of Walter Keane's Big Eye paintings only without the set look of wistful longing.

Hassan did what most men do at a time like that — used the back of his hand to wipe at the pink lipstick smeared on his mouth.

"David—"

"Keep your mouth shut, Greta. I'm feeling pretty hairy right about now. I feel like leaping over that coffin and tearing you apart, and I don't mean your goddam undies this time. So don't trigger me."

"Look here, Ferris," Hassan said in a reasonable tone that was nearly impersonal. "I can appreciate your emotion, but you won't gain anything by being abusive in your —"

"You shut up too, Arab boy. I'll flush you when I want to hear from you. Did you say abusive, you sonofabitch? Jesus. Look what's happened to me ever since you decided you needed a patsy and Greta selected me as sap of the year."

He shook his head impatiently.

"I have no idea what you're talking about, Ferris. But it strikes me you're being very foolish to waste your time in here while Hamel Kebir's men are tracking you down."

"I'm not sweating Hamel any more, sweetheart. I'm handing him over to you and that whore you were just frenching."

"I still don't know what you're talking about and I doubt if you do either."

"Murder, baby. One, two, three, in a row like clay pigeons, and all carefully slated with my name. You just finished unraveling the mystery of the missing mummy by connecting the facts in a logical pattern. Well, now you can listen to the little pattern I've stitched together." I glanced at Greta.

"The build-up must have been about the same as the one the bitch gave me. She hated Papa, she loved you. But Papa wouldn't give her a divorce with cash and what good is a grass widow without a settlement, and why should he be allowed to toss her back to the cathouse where he found her and go on living in style with his four hundred thou? The answer to the problem is so obvious it runs out like a rabid dog and bites you on the leg. Papa has got to go while Greta is still married to him. But it might look odd if he suddenly drops dead and you pop up and claim the wealthy widow. It would look much better if some dummy could be conned into killing him — and get caught at it."

I smiled at him.

"I was the lucky boy. My reputation was sick, I was sitting in poky without a pot to pit in, and all Greta had to do was spread her legs a little because I was the kind of squirrel who would dive in blind. But there was a hitch. Cobb was spying on the side for Brandt, and he must have found out about you and Greta while you were in Cairo. And the pattern says you *knew* he had found out.

"So that wouldn't do. Cobb had to be eliminated before

Brandt was killed. Otherwise — if murder was established or even suspected —.he could show that you and Greta were holding the true motive. It was time for the action. You slipped Cobb some apocynin that night in Luxor, and then you palmed off that phoney vial of nitroglycerin on the potted proctologist to get us out of town without an autopsy. And, fearing that sooner or later some bright boy might do an autopsy and find the bad news in Cobb's stiff, you salted my socks with some spare kernels of the junk. What the hell. Might as well swing me for two murders as one, huh?"

"You're guessing, Ferris."

"Sure. But connect the facts. Other than Brandt who hired him, who else except you had access to Cobb's background? He passed himself off on us as a government survey man, when actually he worked for the Antiquities Service — which is directly connected with your department. So you certainly knew he was playing a dual role."

"You're fumbling wildly in the dark. The fact that I knew who he was proves nothing as far as murder is concerned. It doesn't even establish complicity."

"I didn't say it proved anything. I'm just showing you my little pattern. My conviction didn't start with Cobb. He's just one of the pieces that happen to fit in. I've got a better one."

"Do tell us what it is, David," Greta said.

Her composure was completely restored now, just like her brassiere. Her expression was incuriously placid, as if she were listening to a speech she had heard before and hadn't found it too interesting the first time.

"Stick around, slut. I'll get to it, step by step." I looked at Hassan again.

"Greta sexed me up to knock over Papa — even pretended to draw you away from the scene of the accident. But, after two sad-assed attempts, I lost my nerve for it, and she turned on the frost. No murder, no nooky. And — still playing the part of the Boob of Egypt — I agreed to take another stab at it. But by this time she had learned not to trust my erratic courage. You and she were alone in the marquee when I tailed Papa into the tomb, and she sent you in after me to see if I would really go through with it.

"I didn't. And you were standing back in the corridor and heard what went on between me and Brandt. And that's when you knew you were going to have to do the deed yourself. You and Greta had probably already thought it might finally come to that, and somewhere along the way you'd palmed my knife in anticipation of such a blessed event."

I paused, studying his darkly intelligent face.

"That business with the clothesline must have been an on-the-spot inspiration, huh? Figuring it just might throw in an element of confusion when you were hurting for time. So you reeled in the line and pitched it out of sight, and stepped into some dark nook when I came barging out of the antechamber like a walleyed bull. Then you slipped in behind Brandt's back and did what I had promised Greta I would do but couldn't."

"As brilliant as your deductions may be, Ferris, they are still nothing but pure supposition."

"That's right. But the clincher is coming, and it tidies up the loose ends. I'm talking about Tawwab."

"Tawwab?"

"Uh-huh. As I see it, there's only one valid reason for his death. He saw something Sunday afternoon that he shouldn't have seen, and you knew he had seen it. It stands out like a black eye on an albino when you think about it. Tawwab didn't see you going *to* the tomb — he saw you *coming out of it.*"

Hassan pursed his thin lips thoughtfully and slipped his slender, surgeon-like hands into his jacket pockets. He said nothing.

"You took a king-size gamble when you knifed Brandt. You gambled I would get bollixed up in the maze and give you time to get out of the tomb ahead of me. And it almost paid off. That's why you didn't wait to see if Brandt was really dead. Which he wasn't. But you didn't know that because you were long gone by the time he started to move again.

"You beat me out of the tomb all right, but you walked smack into disaster. Tawwab was coming toward the tomb as you reached the top of the steps, and I was coming out just behind you. So you whipped around and pretended you were coming down. It was a neat trick and I fell for it — but Tawwab knew better and that was why he had to die. How did you get him out there in the ravine? A little flash of money?"

Hassan's aquiline face was as stoical as one of those old

brown portraits of Richelieu you see in Europe's art galleries.

"Tawwab," he said quietly, "was not quite the slavish menial he pretended to be. He was actually a very avaricious man. He suggested a rather exorbitant sum for his silence — but fortunately he was as gullible as he was greedy, or he would have realized I never had any intention of paying blackmail."

"Hassan —" Greta's voice was a hushed warning.

"It's all right, my dear," he told her calmly. "There's no point in trying to maintain our subterfuge with Ferris now. He has done a very creditable job through deduction. And though I fail to see where he has a shred of actual evidence to substantiate his theory, still — he could start our friend Hamel on the right track. Unless of course —"

He was as fast as a cobra. The only mistake he had made was in warning me of that pepper pot a few days before. That's why I had stayed in the doorway — in anticipation.

I saw the sudden flash of that nickel-plated cannon in his upswinging fist and I took a right now backward jump. My heel banged one of those bastardly stones we had cast aside, spinning and dumping me to one knee and both hands just as that revolver went *wowmm* over my head — having in that equilibrium-shattered moment a brief blurred glimpse of Greta's white face with her mouth open and yelling something but I couldn't hear what — and then I was going away in a running crouch like a jack rabbit breaking cover.

19

Across the chamber and through the doorway and down the corridor, and thank God I dodged into the first archway on the left because that gun slammed another earthquake of sound through the tomb and he must have had it centered on my tingling back.

Still going, I flicked on the flashlight, thinking, If this christly passage is a dead-end I'll claw the walls. It wasn't, and it ducked left again and I went with it. Then there was a twenty-foot keyhole bore and I hunched through it and came out in a large chamber with another small tunnel in the opposite wall.

There was a sound. A moment before the tomb had been as still as a North Dakota morgue at midnight. Now a suggestion of unseen movement destroyed the silence with a little scrape and a squeak.

The sound of a shoe? Probably. Hassan had seen me dodge into the puzzle passages, and he would come after me because he was armed and I wasn't. And because he had everything to gain by it and nothing to lose.

He couldn't be too cautious because he was desperately short of time. The echoes of the shots might have been heard by the others out in the camp. Or would they think it was only some loose stones falling in the tomb and who cares?

I wet my lips and snigged off the flash and crouched down at the mouth of the tunnel I had just crawled from, and waited for him to come after me.

The sound came again, and it made others. Some of them seemed to simulate dragging footsteps and all of them — probably crossing certain hollow parts of the stone flooring — made a noise like a faintly muttering, almost ghostly, echo. Real and yet unreal. Impossible to pin down. Like that famous tree which is forever falling in the lonely valley when no one is there to see it fall and no one knows if it made a noise.

It bugged me. I kept trying to hear it, and thinking I did but couldn't tell where it came from. The stale black air went on around me without a hitch and a queer sensation crept over me, something apart from my nervousness and fatigue. A feeling of evil seemed to cloak the dismal tomb, a kind of repugnance mixed with fear, causing the sort of shudder a man might experience on brushing against a leper or standing before an empty house with the blinds drawn on a mysterious street. There was something about that drafty emptiness of stone that was horrific. I wanted to run, to make a lot of noise and get out of there.

Goddammit, something homicidal *had* to be hunkering in the blackness with me, watching me with baleful eyes, waiting for me to make a move, ready to pounce.

This common phenomenon of perspective became so exaggerated I was nearly stupefied by the tremendous effort my reason was making to keep me from pressing the panic button. My tongue swabbed at my dry lips. I breathed deeply, pushing air to the bottom of my lungs. And I kept looking around, trying to *feel* rather than see what might be stealing out of the dark, slow, sure, smiling.

There was no sound now. A weird, expectant hush filled the chamber. The silence grew, like a good-god monster coming mutely and terrifically from a pit.

I saw something.

A quick dull wink of light, on and off before I could swear to it. Like one of those sudden darting flicker impressions you get in the corner of your eye, and when you shoot a look in that direction nothing is ever there.

But I was certain Hassan was there. Not in the chamber with me, not yet, but somewhere back in the tunnel in the opposite wall. Of course it had to be the other tunnel, the one I couldn't reach in time to clobber him with the flash when he came out. That was one of the rules too.

I quarterturned on my heels and put out my left hand as a guide and started back through the keyhole bore. Mister Murder not only had that revolver over me, but we were playing his game as well. He had probably been crawling around in Egyptian tombs for years, tracking down crafty Copt and Arab thieves. I should be duck soup for him.

My feet found some rising steps and I snapped on the flash, pointing it to strike straight upwards to see where they would take me. That abrupt play of light and shadow gave me a second's bad shock. I thought I saw a man rearing up at the head of the stairs.

It was only a wall painting of Anubis, the watchdog of the dead.

I turned the shaft of light in a half circle, looking into the fleeing shadows for the mistakes I could make in the dark. I was shaking now. That moment's pause released my joints and muscles, making me tremble like a vase in an earthquake. When I tried to control it my body seemed to resist, as if it had a will of its own and had decided to give up and get itself shot full of holes.

Move, gutless bastard!

I started up the stairs. My boots, lifting with a scrape from step to step, started an echo series. It was a double

134

sound, as if someone were following me. The insistent realness of this impression spooked me and I took the last seven steps in a rush, spun about at the top, splashed the light below me and saw the staircase was empty.

The relaxation of my nerves — some still tense, some half eased, all of them somewhat awry — gave me an exhilaration of courage that was as false as Greta's marriage vows. But it was better than nothing to go on.

Stepping into an ascending passage, the flash showed me the white stripe of the clothesline running north and south on the floor. I was back on the mainline. I thumbed off the light and started up the passage. But not far. Only six or seven feet in the dark, and then I got that illusion of the double sound again. The echo — mine — tangled itself with some vague undertone suggesting a separate parallel movement: stopping when I stopped, moving when I moved.

Just before I reached the wide drainwater pit the illusion became so persistent I turned around and shot a beam of light down the corridor. Nothing. Just the foetor-clad rock walls and a dense pool of blackness beyond the flashlight's limit of penetration.

I doused the light and turned and took one-two steps and started to take the third but caught it in midair, and listened.

Behind me — *scuff scuff scuff*. Three times.

He was stalking me and he was so close I could almost smell him.

Another staircase was right ahead of me and I went up it blind, in a hurry, and along a short horizontal passage, and then I was standing on the bridge over the forty-foot deep drainpit.

The bridge the *fellahs* had built was a simple construction: two long eight by thirteens spanning the gap, with short lengths of two by twelve for planking. It was five feet wide, no rails, and each end lay well inside the mouth of a passageway.

I played my light in a wide circle around the pit and saw that the lower portion of the walls — at a level with the bridge and the footing of the two opposing doorways — was completely corbeled with an encircling rampstone. The top of this projection was perfectly flat and one foot wide.

All right. It was time for the gutless wonder to take a stand.

I eased myself around one corner of the wall, put my left foot on the corbel ramp, my left cheek and jittery gut flat against the clammy stone wall, and inched myself along until I had room for my right foot on the ramp too. Then I froze, both arms stretched up and out from my sides like a man crucified on his stomach instead of his back. I snicked off the light and gripped the flash by the butt in my right hand, only a few inches from the corner of the doorway.

Then I waited in the listening dark.

It seemed to me I waited a long time before I heard the hushed *scuff scuff* of his footsteps coming along the passage.

His flashlight glowed tentatively in the rectangular opening by my side. Then it brightened, became brilliant, and tossed a diamond-like dazzle on the planked bridge just below me and on the shadowy walls standing back and away from me.

I watched it expand in brilliance, chasing leaping shadows on ahead, sending them scurrying into blind corners, shooting them up the walls of the shaft and plunging them down into the mucky depths of the drainpit.

My sweaty hand felt as if I were holding a slimy dead eel. I pulled it out from the wall and cocked the flash like a Neanderthal man aiming a club at a hairy enemy or at the gaggly female he wanted for a mate.

And the light kept getting brighter and brighter, and still he didn't step through the opening, and I got so squirrely with anticipation and anxiety I started praying again. Please dear Jesus God in heaven let him believe I've already crossed the bridge and make him step right out on it and give me a fair crack at him because if he spots me first —

Thummp.

He had stepped onto the planks. He was just around the corner and in another two steps . . .

I sucked air and clenched my teeth and leaned to the left — and in that last vivid split second something that sprang out of pure primordial savagery screamed inside me.

136

I'll kill every sonofabitch in the world!

He stepped through the opening, the revolver in his right hand, the flashlight in his left, and the darkness took a wild tilt and sprang behind him. For one static moment his profile was as clearly defined as if it had been clipped out of black tin.

I swung the flashlight at it.

Everything I had went into that swing, and I felt the *whonk* of the blow on his temple ripple up my arm to my neck like an electric shock, and then I was thrown off balance and taking that dreamlike bowelless plunge into space, hearing — abstractly — the heavy revolver clatter-bounce on the planks as I fell after a careening shadow-chased light.

The planks slammed into my gut, chest, chin and I fingerclawed and clung to them like a nymphomaniac climbing a lover in the dark.

But it wasn't totally dark. A faint crepuscular light was casting a ghostly glow somewhere below me, beyond the opposite edge of the planks. I got all of me up on the bridge and crawled over to the other side and looked down.

The bottom of the drainpit was mud. Hassan's flashlight had broken through the hardened top crust and was three-fourths buried. The little oval of light that still gleamed determinedly was centered on a dark prostrate shape.

Forty feet is a long way to fall. His body was sprawled face-down in that stinking viscous muck, arms out, legs drawn up. It didn't look like a body from where I was. It looked like a monstrous crushed gray frog, its innards crawling and seeping into a black stagnant pool.

Another light glittered behind me and I heard feet move rapidly on the planks and then stop.

I stood up and looked around, and the crystalline glare of a flashlight caught me squarely in the eyes, blinding me on the spot. Greta's voice hissed out of the darkness like a striking pltviper.

"You filthy sonofabitch!"

I tried to shield my eyes with a splayed hand but I still couldn't make her out. She kept that dazzling whorl of light on my face. I didn't know where my flashlight had gone and I wondered if she had found Hassan's revolver, and if she had if she would know how to use it.

137

"Why did you have to kill him? You couldn't kill any-one else. Why couldn't it be *you* down there? I loved him, goddam you!"

I wet my lips amd made a step nearer, batting my eyes against that blaze of light. A person who isn't used to re-volvers will usually forget to cock the hammer, which makes a stiff pull on the trigger causing it to jerk high when fired.

"Greta —"

"Shut up! I can't stand the sight or sound of you. You couldn't kill Farley. Oh no, not a pig like that. But you killed *him* — the only man I ever gave a damn about! He was clean and intelligent and kind. He didn't stink of gin and sweat or have dirt under his fingernails or talk like a Madison Avenue Babbitt. He wasn't a stupid little two-bit thief. He had courage. And *you* killed him. You — a nothing, a scum, a tool for anyone to use. Did you really think I loved you? Did you actually believe *I could?* My God!"

Her laugh was high and loud, hysterical, and when I heard it I knew I had to get my hands on her, on her neck, and wring the mockery out of her. I had thought I wanted to kill Farley Brandt, but I couldn't. And after he was dead I was sorry. I had killed Hassan in self-defense, but I hadn't hated him. And I was sorry about him too. But now I was finally ready to join that alien clan who have separated themselves from the brotherhood of man by willfully destroying human life.

I hated her, and the passion was stronger than reason.

I took another step, not trying to protect my eyes from the blinding light now, staring fixedly above it at the place where her throat would be.

Go!

I bent my knees, throwing my body forward, and took off in an abrupt tearing rush.

A burst of orange flame spat from the whorling white light and my eardrums clanged like clashing cymbals. Something stopped me short and I stood transfixed for a brief moment, gawking and smelling the acrid stench of cordite fumes. Then I began to laugh.

Missed! Sweet Christ I win!

I started forward again, still laughing. My mouth was

full of something salty and warm and I tried to cough, to spit it out, but I didn't have a chance.

Dawn was coming up and I was in a hurry to meet it.

20

MY LEFT side was acting up. It felt as if some damn fool had spilled a pan of boiling soup over it.

"Jesus," I said.

I opened my eyes and a lantern was radiating a hazy light by my head. I worked my lids a few times and the haze dissipated. My face was on the bridge planking and I could see each separate little wooden splinter and each one cast its own small shadow.

Greta's face was five feet away from me.

She was lying on the planks too, her eyes open but not quite looking at or seeing me. They looked the way they always did, very green and reserved and careful, except that I could see they had become fixed in the depths of their dark holes by the gleam of white becoming steady there. Then I knew what was wrong with them.

"Jesus," I said.

"Remain very still, Mr. Ferris, please. I am trying to stop the bleeding in your back. It appears to be a nice clean wound. It went in little and came out larger."

It was Hamel's voice and he was speaking over my head. Until then I hadn't been consciously aware of his fingers fiddling in the hot soup on my back. I couldn't see him.

I saw Jeff Wren. He was standing by the wall just beyond Greta's huddled body. He looked drawn and tired, sunken in, like a man with a prolonged illness and too stubborn to go to bed with it. He was staring at Greta. Then he looked at me.

When he first spoke his voice was as flat as a rug. Then it started to go uphill, rushing toward uncontrolled hysteria.

"I killed her, Dave. She was standing with her back to me and I saw her shoot you. Somebody had left a shovel in the corridor and I picked it up. Maybe at first I thought I was only going to stun her with it. But when I raised it over my head and had her standing right there in front of me I suddenly knew I was going to crush her! Had to smash her like glass! And I brought it down with every —"

"Mr. Wren," Hamel said in a crisp voice. "Would you please go find some of the *fellahs?* Have them make some kind of stretcher for Mr. Ferris. And please ask Dr. Ferber to drive into town for an ambulance."

Jeff responded like a hysteric who had just received a slap in the face to shut him up. He stood very still and blinked his agitated eyes at Hamel.

"Yes," he muttered.

I listened to his footsteps recede, leaving behind the double sound.

"Now then. Do you think you can roll over, Mr. Ferris? I must see to your front side. I'm using Mrs. Brandt's halfslip for bandaging. That's rather poetic justice, don't you agree?"

He helped me onto my back. It didn't hurt too much. I was starting to feel numb and I was afraid I was going to pass out again. I had something important to say first.

"Look. About what Jeff Wren just said —"

"I don't think you should try to talk, Mr. Ferris. In any event, I've been so busy with my policeman's first aid that I really didn't hear a word Mr. Wren said. As far as I am officially concerned, Mr. Wren did a very commendable act. Fearing that Mrs. Brandt intended to shoot you again, he stopped her by hitting her with a shovel. It is certainly not his fault that he hit a little too hard."

I smiled and closed my eyes. He was a pretty good little guy.

They got me in my tent and on my cot, and Anne fussed around and fretted about my bandage until Hamel made a polite suggestion that she should let me get some rest. Doc had already taken off for Aswan to fetch me a doctor and an ambulance.

Anne gave a damp-eyed, sisterly smile.

"I'm so glad it wasn't you, Dave. I really am."

140

"Wasn't me what?"

"You know — Mr. Brandt and the others. Mr. Kebir's told me that Greta and Hassan planned the entire thing, and that he never did really suspect you."

I looked up at Hamel, at his little pleased baby smile.

"He did pretty good at keeping it a secret." I felt bitter.

"But I still can't understand how Hassan could do such terrible things. He seemed like such a nice man. Such a refined gentleman."

It was easy to understand if you were a man and if you had known Greta. The foolish very young and the foolish very old. She got to them all.

"Everyone seems like a nice man to you," I said. "I'm going to have to talk to you about that sometime."

She gave me a pat and another smile and went away. I didn't care. I looked at the fat little detective."

"Why didn't you suspect me?"

"Well, perhaps it's a seventh sense I have. I really can't say. But there was something about you, Mr. Ferris, that didn't smack of the killer breed. You seemed too apprehensive, too harassed, too angry. You reminded me of a man who had been used as a dupe and who found out about it when it was too late. And I let you continue thinking along that line because it fit my purpose to do so."

"What was your purpose?"

"I had a feeling that if the guilty party — or parties, as it turned out — thought I believed you were guilty, they would start to relax, lower their defense and allow me a glimpse of their motive. That is why I let you run. It gave me a valid excuse to remove the watchful presence of the law from the scene of the crime."

"You took a big chance, didn't you? How did you know I wouldn't kill you when you let me slug you? You couldn't have been certain that I hadn't killed Brandt."

He shrugged his plump shoulders.

"A bit of a chance, perhaps. But not much. You see, I *was* certain you hadn't killed him. Only a stupid person would leave his knife in the back of the man he has murdered. And you didn't strike me as being very stupid, Mr. Ferris. Then, of course, when I found the apocynin seeds in your socks I was positive you were being framed."

"Worse than you think. I found Tawwab's body last night in a ravine. He was strangled with one of my belts."

Hamel threw up his stubby hands in a gesture of despair.

"You see? No doubt Hassan Bey was very intelligent in his own field. But when it came to murder his methods were much too obvious."

"You knew it was Hassan?"

"N-o. Not positively. But he seemed to fit the pattern better than anyone else. And then I knew I was right when I heard what Mrs. Brandt said to you just before she shot you."

"You heard all that? You were there?"

"Back in the dark with Mr. Wren. Yes. We had heard gunshots in the tomb and we came in to see who was making them and why. Unfortunately, Mrs. Brandt had her back to us and appeared only as a silhouette. We didn't know she had a pistol until you so foolishly tried to rush her. Can you forgive me for taking a risk with your life? It was essential that I heard what she had to say because I had hinged my entire case on her."

"Why not?" I said. "What's a bullet hole between *amigos?*"

He beamed at me. "So nice of you to adopt that attitude, Mr. Ferris. Well, well. I think I'd better wait outside until the doctor arrives. You need rest."

"I need morphine a hell of a lot more. This damn thing is burning like fire. Tell Jeff I want to see him a minute, huh?"

Jeff came into the tent by himself and lit us both a cigarette and put mine in my mouth. He was still looking as if he were twice his actual age and didn't know where he would find the pep to make up for the change.

"Jeff, did Greta try to get you to kill Farley?"

"Yeah. Last year when we were shacking for a couple of weeks."

He stared at his cigarette, watching the smoke curl away.

"I was crazy about her — but I couldn't do that. And she knew it, so she threw me over. I should have scrammed. If I'd had any sense, I would have. But I couldn't bring myself to leave her. I hung around like a sad-ass lovelorn schoolboy. Anything to be near her. But the longer I stayed the more my hate grew." He looked at me.

"The funny thing is, I never really admitted to myself that I did hate her. It wasn't until I had that shovel in my

142

hands and raised it over her head that . . ." He made a noise in his throat and doused his cigarette.

I didn't say anything, but I knew exactly how he felt. That was why I had rushed her. It had been time to get out of the Round Robin Club.

"I don't know what Hamel will do about it," he said in a dull voice. "Maybe he'll decide to pin a murder on me. He heard what I said to you in the tomb."

"He's not going to do anything about it, Jeff. He told me he didn't hear a word you said."

His face flashed a look of renewed interest.

"Really? Huh! Funny little guy, isn't he? You know what I saw him do in the tomb? He happened to spot a quartz scarab back in a dark corner while the boys were lowering you down from the gallery. I saw him pick it up. It was about the size of a fifty-cent piece with little gold legs. Tomb robbers must have dropped it on their way out. Know what he did? Slipped it in his pocket, just like a common thief. It must be something atavistic in people, huh?"

The pain was growing wicked now. I wet my lips and stared up at the flies clustered on the ceiling of the tent.

"Yeah. In all of us. One way or another."

But I didn't want to talk about it. I closed my eyes and put Greta and all of them out of my mind. I thought about that ambulance Doc was bringing. What was the use of worrying? It never was worth while.

143